Bentota

KAI HENRY

BENTOTA

Publisher: BoD · Books on Demand, Östermalmstorg 1,
114 42 Stockholm, Sweden, bod@bod.se
Printer: Libri Plureos GmbH, Friedensallee 273,
22763 Hamburg, Germany
ISBN: 978-91-8114-497-0

PREFACE

I have always had trouble falling asleep at night. Everyone has heard of counting sheep jumping over fences, but I've never understood it. Is it supposed to be monotonous with all the sheep being the same – black or white, big or small? Why would you get tired from seeing lively sheep? I've probably tried, but in my counting, one of them always falls over or the crown jewels hit the fence, and they end up lying there writhing in pain.

No, instead, I started many years ago during sleepless evenings and nights to embark on a fantasy journey. It developed over time, and I could jump right into the "next episode" without missing a beat. It helped, and I slept better. It eventually became quite a long story. I told a friend about it after years of "fantasy traveling." He thought it definitely should be written down. I left it at that, but after years of contemplation, I gathered the courage to contact an author who shared the same opinion my friend had years earlier. She is a Finnish-Swedish author who has published three books, Mia Bergenheim. I live in Thailand myself but made a detour to Finland, where we met and almost immediately started working on the book. I wrote first and sent a few pages to Mia, who then rewrote them to make the text more "book-style." We had probably made it halfway through the book when Mia thought I should write the book myself. It probably differed so much from her previous books that she had some difficulty understanding what I wanted. Or perhaps she grew tired of my complaining and correcting the text she wrote. But by then, I had caught the writing bug and restarted in my own rough style. However, without Mia's encouragement and help, the book probably would never have come to be.

The story takes place 150 years in the future, in the year 2174. Yep, we're heading out into space and the unknown – or maybe not. Read on to find out. But if you're a space geek and want to know how things work in the future, you should stop here. I don't know anything about that, and maybe someone knows what the world will look like 150 years from now? My dad used to say, "It's hard to predict, and especially hard to predict the future."

But imagine you are a leader with 1,600 people, and you have to start a new world. How many things from today's world would you want to bring along? Money, cell phones, cars, credit cards, swimming pools, nice clothes, luxury food, restaurants, movies, TV, stereos, beer, spirits, cigarettes? No, that's what I would answer to that – you need yourself and your fellow human beings.

A big thank you to my mom as well, who has supported me and been happy to see me follow in my grandfather's footsteps, who was a writer. I hope he won't be turning in his grave when he reads the book.

1. HOTEL KÄMP

I looked out the window at a bleak autumn-winter landscape, slushy and wet. I was furious and out of sorts, so the gray weather fit my mood well. They said the hotel was located right in the center of Helsinki and was the best place to hold the annual conference organized by ICPA (International Corrections & Prisons Association). I had been asked on short notice to act as host for the event. Although I had been a board member for several years, everyone knew that these events were something I did not look forward to. But since all the others were, oddly enough, unavailable – plus a few "convenient" colds – I didn't have much choice when the chairman of the board asked me to take care of it.

Sure, I didn't mind the actual travel; HQ was in Brussels, but I was rarely there. So now I flew directly from my home in New York, and with the new electric jets, the trip took no more than four hours. The jet lag was worse than the flight. Especially when flying west, it always felt strange to arrive a few hours before you even started. No, there was nothing wrong with the travel or the hotel, which was almost 300 years old. Built back in 1887, Hotel Kämp was considered one of the best in the Nordics. That wasn't what was gnawing at me. It was the new correctional reform I was trying to get implemented to the "dinosaurs" in corrections.

I had developed a system that would allow us to implant microchips in everyone, not just the elite. With the ongoing refugee influx, we had no chance of controlling crime worldwide. I had a sense that the already microchipped elite were quite satisfied with their lives. They got to live in their enclosed areas with armed guards and every comfort. But what kind of freedom was it if you couldn't go to the beach, have a family picnic, or even take a car trip without, at best, just being robbed? The world had become a dangerous place for everyone.

So after my lecture in the hotel's Hall of Mirrors, I felt empty. I received my obligatory applause; someone asked a question about the subject, but otherwise, it seemed like people were more interested in the drinks and buffet. I could have ended the lecture with the classic line, "Any questions, or should we start drinking?" Tomorrow's schedule included group work and an excursion to a prison classified as "high security." I was starting to get tired of these excursions and meetings that led nowhere. I chose a bottle of Chivas Regal from the minibar, lay comfortably on the bed, and reflected on my life.

I would soon turn 45, with no children, not even a girlfriend since Cynthia and I broke up almost a year ago. We saw no reason to continue since we were both constantly traveling – she in medical research and I with my work. We broke up over a phone call, with no drama or anything like that. I don't think we'd seen each other for a month when we decided it would be for the best. It had been over six months since I last saw my parents. They lived in a nice suburban area in New Jersey, mostly digging around in their garden. I had promised to come over for Christmas dinner, which wasn't too far off, so I'd get to ease my guilty conscience for a while.

2. A WALK IN HELSINKI

I decided to take a short walk despite the weather. It was November, and winter was approaching, but there was hardly any snow yet. The center of Helsinki was classified as a "Go Zone" as opposed to all the "No-Go Zones" that existed all over the world. I walked a few hundred meters and eventually stepped into a souvenir shop, thinking I might find something nice for Mom since I'd promised to come over for Christmas. I picked out a Santa Claus on a sled with reindeer in front of him. I thought Santa must have a lot of work these days, given that the world population was around 12 billion. I turned the number over in my head for a while – 12 billion, the same as 12 thousand million people. What was going to happen? It wasn't sustainable in any form. It felt hopeless, and at the same time, I couldn't shake the feeling that all the work I'd done was meaningless. Nothing could be stopped anymore with the resources available.

I walked back to the hotel, feeling, if possible, even more depressed. "Mr. Carter, you have a message; the code is in your room," called the receptionist. I thanked her and took the elevator to my room. I tossed the Santa with Rudolph and the other reindeer into my bag, took the code, and threw myself onto the bed. "Play code a34b75." I heard

Ralph's voice: "John, call me as soon as you've listened to the message." What could it be now, I wondered, probably some last-minute changes to the program, I assumed. Ralph was my boss and also the chairman of ICPA, so there wasn't much to do except call him back.

"Call Ralph Wilkins, ICPA." Ralph answered in just a few seconds. "Sorry to bother you, John," said Ralph. "No worries, it's not like I'm lying by the pool sunbathing," I replied. Ralph didn't laugh at my joke but continued, "You have to go to Helsinki Airport tomorrow morning. There's a private jet waiting to take you to Fort Lauderdale. WSA wants to speak with you." "WSA?" I blurted out, "World Space Association? What do they want – do they want me to build a prison on the moon?" "I only know it's a top priority, so you mustn't mention this to anyone, understood?" Ralph continued. "Understood, of course, but the seminar…" I started. "I've delegated everything to Tom, so you don't need to worry about it. Make sure you're in the lobby by 8 tomorrow morning. An escort will take you to the airport." "An escort…" I started to ask. "That's all I know. Make sure you get a good night's sleep; I think you'll need it for tomorrow. That's all from me, goodnight, John." "Yes, goodbye," I replied, and the call ended. No small talk, just straight to the point. What the hell was this all about, I wondered.

Getting to sleep after that conversation was not going to be easy. I had another glass of Chivas and thought it over for a while, but it didn't help much. Sure, there was some relief in skipping tomorrow's monotonous program in a slushy Helsinki and trading it for sunny Florida. Maybe it was some entirely new project – almost anything sounded appealing now. Against all odds, I slept quite well anyway.

3. TIME ZONES

Even though I travel a lot, I've never liked flying westward. We took off at exactly 9:00 from Helsinki and landed at Cape Canaveral's private airfield four hours later at 6:00. But arriving three hours before I had even started always amazed me. The new hyper-fast electric jets were comfortable, and having it all to myself didn't hurt either. I had eaten at the hotel in the morning and slept well, so I wasn't the least bit tired or hungry. A car met me at the plane, and from a distance, I could see the towering rocket structures that launched almost daily towards the moon base – carrying tourists, researchers, and other personnel. Moon tourism had started a few decades ago but had lost some prestige as it was only accessible to the elite who could afford the exorbitant prices.

Massive protests were often held outside the base, with incidents of gunfire and even fatalities. It was something I understood well, given my involvement with such issues. The population was reaching its breaking point; most of Earth's people lived on the brink of starvation. The whole situation was unsustainable, and there was no solution in sight – not even remotely close.

The car took me to a low building, and the driver told me my room number and said he'd pick me up in two hours. I tried to get some information out of him, but he said he was just following orders and didn't know anything else. I raised my wrist where I had my implanted chip card, and the door unlocked. "Room number 5 is yours, Mr. Carter," said a pleasant female voice over the speaker. I entered the room, tossed my bag on the bed, and took a quick shower for the second time today. The room was simple but comfortable. I grabbed an orange juice from the fridge and flopped onto the bed to gather my thoughts.

I figured it was pointless to ask the screen any questions – it wouldn't lead anywhere. WSA, what could they want with my expertise? Could it be possible they needed a holding facility for troublesome workers on the moon or an overindulgent tourist? It seemed far-fetched since only top-tier experts even had a chance of applying for a job on the moon base. They also organized moonwalks for tourists, for a hefty fee that could feed hundreds of people. So, it was hard to believe that any of the lucky few who could afford it would ruin their unique experience by getting drunk and causing a scene on the moon base.

I tried not to think about it and instead to take a little nap. But that turned out to be futile; too many thoughts were swirling in my head now. It was just a matter of waiting until 8:00 for the car to pick me up. Soon enough, I'd get answers to my questions. Right at 8:00, I saw the same car with the same driver pull up in front of the door from the window. I hadn't seen any other people today, so it was almost like meeting an old acquaintance. The sun had already risen, and it was pleasantly warm. It had now been six hours since I left the dark, slushy Helsinki behind.

4. WSA

I was escorted by the quiet driver through what I assumed was the main entrance to the WSA Kennedy Space Center. WSA was known as NASA about a hundred years ago but changed its name when several countries pooled their expertise and funding to allow for larger projects and better opportunities to explore the unknown. It hadn't been easy for WSA, as most people opposed the enormous billion-dollar investments in projects that didn't seem to lead anywhere. Sure, they had established bases on both Mars and the Moon, but that hardly helped or comforted people who couldn't afford their daily meals. Rumors had been circulating about a massive spaceship under construction, and clear signs of it were the increasingly frequent trips between the Moon and Earth – this had been going on for years now and was making people nervous as no clear answers were given.

I was led into a conference room with a large round table where five people were seated, though there was enough space for 25 more. Everyone stood up and came over to greet me. First was Craig Thomas, the leading figure at WSA. I had seen him countless times in news bulletins and debates, passionate about space research and trying to defend WSA's vast budgets. Recently, however, he had been in the news less often, as the pressure on WSA kept increasing. "Thank you for coming, John, and I apologize for our clumsy kidnapping." "It's fine," I replied. "Florida's warmth as an excuse to escape Finland's winter works for me." Everyone laughed and introduced themselves quickly.

We sat down, and Craig began, "You probably have a lot of questions, and we'll answer them all in due time, but first, a question for you: how is your project with ICPA and the chipping of the population progressing?"

"Mr. Thomas," I began, but he interrupted me right away. "Just Craig, if you don't mind – we don't do formalities among our own." "Thank you, Craig," I replied, thinking, *among our own? What on earth did he mean by that?* I continued, "To be honest, it's like spitting into the wind in a storm. ICPA sees it as a good solution, but I've started to realize the project is unsustainable. It would simply take too long, plus there's significant resistance, especially from the poorest people. They see it as a threat to their freedom, and in part, they're right. Since I initiated the project, I have to bite the bullet and admit that, at least on the scale it's intended, it's not going to succeed."

"Thank you for your honesty," Craig replied. "It's about what we expected." Then he turned to another person, "Anders, can you take over for a moment? John is starting to look like a living question mark."

"Yes, hi, I'm Anders Lind, originally from Sweden, so I totally understand why you'd rather be here than in Finland. But I'm the project leader for something that's going to take your breath away. We've found an Earth-like planet where we plan to send 1,600 people to establish a colony – 800 Adams and 800 Eves. We've built a spaceship over the past 30 years from the moon base, hence the intense rocket traffic in recent years. And now we're in a rush; we have conflicts all over the world, and there's a risk everything will fall apart if we don't get going soon."

The room suddenly felt very warm. "Sorry to interrupt, but everything you're saying sounds incredible. What does this have to do with me?" Everyone stared at me seriously until Anders dropped the bomb. "John, we want you to lead the group."

"Uh, what? No… no, no, no. Is this a joke?" Now I was starting to feel seriously uncomfortable. Craig rescued me, saying, "Let's take 10 minutes here; Anders, stay behind." I stood up as well, poured mineral water into a glass, and downed it. I took a few deep breaths and tried to make sense of things. "Can you go over that one more time, Anders? I don't think I heard you correctly." "Your reaction is exactly what we expected, but we couldn't think of a better way. It would have been tricky over email." "Yes, it would've gone straight to spam," I replied.

For the next two hours, I was briefed on the most astounding project the world had ever witnessed. The first moon landing in 1969 must have been an enormous event for people back then. But this was something completely different; a moon landing paled in comparison to what these people were planning. I had no intention whatsoever of participating in the project.

5. VIRIDIS

After a two-hour lecture with many interruptions due to my questions, I had gathered enough information to get an overall picture. Quasitor 3, a massive spaceship nearly 900 meters long, had been constructed over 30 years from parts shipped via the moon base. Quasitor 3 was the same ship as Quasitor 1 and 2, but after improvements and test flights in space, they had renamed it with each iteration. The biggest shock came when I asked how long the journey would take. "It's final," Craig said. "The journey itself will take 400 years to reach Viridis, which is what we've named it. It means 'green' in Latin, and since Earth is called 'the blue planet,' why not." "You can see images on the screen to understand what I mean." The planet was indeed very green, so vegetation was abundant. It also had a lot of blue, though not large oceans like we have on Earth.

Craig continued, "The journey will be done in two stages: you'll be put into stasis and awakened after 200 years for a month of rehabilitation and recovery, then another 200-year stage until you arrive." "Oh," I managed, hoping I hadn't left my mouth hanging open while he explained. "But how safe is this stasis?" I couldn't believe I was even asking the question, but the whole story was fascinating. "The journey as a whole is relatively safe; stasis carries about a one-in-a-thousand risk of someone not waking up, so we expect that one or two people, unfortunately, may not survive the trip. But I can tell you that all five of us in this room have tested stasis for periods from two weeks up to six months. Jack, of course, wanted to stay the longest."

"Didn't want to miss Christmas; otherwise, I'd have stayed as long as possible," Jack laughed. Jack Wiggum was one of the minds behind "Linda," the hypercomputer that ran everything in the project. Linda was the world's most powerful computer and also made a crew unnecessary on the ship. Ralph continued, "You'll get to meet Linda's twin sister today, Leyla, onboard Quasitor." "What?" I blurted out again, like some country bumpkin. "Didn't you say the ship was in space?" "We have an exact replica here to address any potential issues," Craig continued. "And you'll also meet another interesting person, but I suggest we have lunch before heading to Quasitor."

I trailed after Craig and the others, feeling completely lost. I felt like a farmer seeing New York for the first time. We arrived at an enormous cafeteria with a ceiling at least 20 meters high. Nothing gourmet, but quick and easy, as everything had to function smoothly with over 20,000 people working here, about half of them on the Quasitor project. "Simple is good," I replied and grabbed some food from the buffet. "When is the departure?" I asked, more out of general interest.

"January 15, 2174, the journey begins, with you on board or without," Craig replied. Just two months left, I calculated; I'd have time to celebrate Christmas with my parents before departure. What the hell was happening – was I actually considering joining the project? "I know what you're thinking, John; I know you have an almost astronomical salary. It would go to your parents as long as they're alive – they could live a very comfortable life after your departure." The thought was appealing; I had a very high salary and was terrible at spending money, so most of it just piled up in the bank. I had always made sure my parents were well taken care of. I was almost always traveling, and ICPA covered the expenses with per diems and other allowances, so my salary remained mostly untouched. I'd considered donating it to those in need, but to whom and where? Corrupt aid organizations didn't interest me. And the whole world was in need, with 90% below subsistence level and nearly 50% of the world's population starving. Yet, the population kept growing by hundreds of millions each year. No one really knew the total population now; 12–12.5 billion was probably a good guess.

Pandemics came and went so quickly we didn't even know which one was currently spreading, and only a fraction received treatment for it. The influx of refugees had been unstoppable for years already. In America alone, the population had reached around 500 million, far more than the original population, and in Europe, the situation was even worse. Farmers had their lands guarded by the military, and they didn't hesitate to use live ammunition. Social services where people could seek help hadn't existed since the early 2100s. It was a hopeless situation; no one trusted politicians anymore. Everyone had their own agenda. The race was almost over. Maybe that's why small ideas began to form in my mind – escaping from all this, starting fresh, doing it right. Without greedy kings, dictators, maybe even free from the entire capitalist mindset.

After lunch, a driverless electric minibus took us to a large building where a gate opened, and we drove up a ramp. We stepped out, and I just stood there staring. "Welcome, Mr. John Carter," said a woman's voice from hidden speakers,

"I've been waiting to meet you. My name is Leyla, and I'm Linda's twin sister." "Just call me John," I managed to say. "Pleasure, John," replied Leyla. Anders added, "Linda – or rather, Leyla in this case – will follow your every command, and her capacity is practically limitless. She handles navigation, controls the air on the ship, monitors those in stasis, provisions – even creates personalized fitness programs for everyone, using the data in their microchip, during your month-long rest after the first 200 years."

"What happens if something goes wrong with her… with Linda?" I asked. "There's only a microscopic chance of that happening," Anders replied. "The main reason we're about five years behind schedule is that we've added countless backup systems. Believe me, we've thought of everything, even the impossible. She will get you to your destination, Viridis. Then it's up to you, the participants."

"But when we said you'd meet an interesting person, we didn't mean Leyla, however fascinating she might be – no offense, Leyla," Craig said. "Not at all," Leyla replied immediately. Craig continued, "No, I meant Miss Riya Mendis," and gestured behind me. I turned around to see an incredibly appealing woman smiling at me. "Pleased to meet you, Mr. John Carter," she said, giving me a firm handshake. "Call me John," I said, feeling myself blush and feeling absurdly embarrassed by it.

Craig took over, "Riya would be your second-in-command and would take over if anything happened to you. Riya is a doctor and holds the rank of lieutenant in the Indian Army, where she trained and taught soldiers survival skills for crisis situations – even performing minor surgeries under primitive conditions. She's tough as nails and trained to handle almost any crisis." "So they say," Riya laughed. "People are always at their best in job interviews." Craig laughed, "Apparently, I was completely fooled." We all laughed, instantly easing the tension.

"We'll leave you two to get acquainted, and Riya can give you a tour of the ship. Are you up for it, John?" Craig asked. "Sure, no problem," I replied. I felt a bit awkward as the five-person delegation left us alone in the enormous ship. "Craig said you're a doctor. I mean, you look so young." "Thank you, but I'm actually 34," she replied. "Well, I wouldn't have guessed. I'm 44, and it definitely shows." "A handsome 44, then," Riya smiled, flashing her white teeth. Damn, I was blushing again.

We sat at a simple table with a few chairs, and a robotic cart came to take our orders. We both chose mineral water, which arrived quickly. "So, Riya, I haven't agreed to the mission yet," I said after a moment. "But you will," she replied with a smile. Damn, she was almost enchanting – not just her smile, but those dark brown, nearly black eyes, and her black hair, which almost shone with a hint of blue.

Riya continued, "As I see it, we don't have a choice. The world is on a fast track to hell. Soon there will be massive uprisings, leading to bloodshed on a scale never seen before. There are strong guerrilla movements within the U.S. and everywhere else in the world. No offense to your prison reforms, but do you really think they have a future?" I leaned forward, resting my hands on my forehead, feeling both tired and old. "You're right on every point, Riya, but how did you handle the issue with your family, friends, and loved ones?"

"Oh, it was an ordeal, of course, but in the end, they realized that this mission is bigger than even that. And WSA's financial support helped too. Both my parents and my two brothers were promised substantial financial help. In India, children are expected to support their parents for life, and it's comforting to know I can still do that even if I never see them again." I could see she was a bit emotional when we talked about her family, and that felt right somehow.

"Well, Riya, ready to give me the grand tour?"

We wandered around the enormous ship as Riya filled me in on the details. Nearly 900 meters long and with three levels, powered by both atomic and solar energy. It was almost like a small city. With a maximum capacity of over 10,000 people, it was clearly built for migration to habitable planets. Now it was about to embark on its first long journey with 1,600 people – possibly sentenced to death or to a life in a new paradise.

We stopped in front of an enormous black block, about 20 meters wide and probably 50 meters long. Riya gestured for me to sit on a sofa, and I noticed there were plenty of similar seating areas scattered around. Cozy corners for socializing.

"Hello, Leyla," said Riya.

"Hello, Riya and John," replied the box.

"Excuse my appearance; I've put on some weight over the years."

"It happens to the best of us," I replied.

"Try her out," Riya suggested.

"How?" I wondered.

"She can do almost anything and knows everything. It's up to you."

"Leyla, can you call Ralph Wilkins at ICPA?" I said.

"Hologram?" Leyla asked.

"Yes, that's fine."

A few seconds later, Ralph appeared a couple of meters in front of us.

"Good evening, Riya and John," Ralph began.

"Oh, so you two know each other," I said, surprised for the thousandth time that day.

"For a few months now," Riya replied. "It's been my task to find a suitable leader for the project. John, you are in a class of your own. If you choose not to participate, I will lead the project, but I want you with us."

Not used to genuine compliments, I tried to deflect.

"Ralph, what do you have to say about all this?"

"If I weren't so damn old, I'd do anything to be part of this. Sure, there are risks with the project, but it's starting to feel like the risks of survival on Earth are even smaller. Just go; I have a feeling this is our last chance. WSA will be the first target of people's anger when the uprisings start. And one more thing, John – your parents know about this!"

"What?" I exclaimed, looking at Riya.

"Yes, I may have talked to them as well," she replied, looking quite uncertain, almost on the verge of tears. I felt sympathy and patted her arm.

"Leyla, can you bring my parents here too?"

After a few seconds, we were five in the "meeting" as my parents joined us.

"Hello, Mom and Dad. Things are a bit strange here."

"Hello, sweetheart," Mom began.

"I understand you're confused," Dad added.

"Yeah, that's an understatement. This morning I was in Helsinki, and now everyone wants me to leave forever."

Mom continued, "No one wants you gone; it's just how things are now. And don't worry about us; we only want what's best for you. You could build something great. Riya explained everything to us. She's a wonderful person – a perfect match for you."

"Mom!" I exclaimed, sure I was blushing like a ripe tomato.

Riya sat beside me, trying to hold back laughter.

"Well, thank you, everyone. As I said, I haven't decided one way or the other. I need time to think. And Mom, Dad, I'll be home for Christmas as planned. And Ralph, do you need anything from me before I…" Damn.

"Yes, goodnight, everyone." The holograms vanished, and I leaned back on the sofa and closed my eyes.

"Would you like a drink?" Riya asked.

"How many is the question. A Chivas to start with."

The robot cart returned with two Chivas Regals. I added ice to the glasses.

"Cheers," I said, taking a sip. "What a day. An information bomb – a shock to the entire system."

We sat in silence for a while until Riya spoke.

"Sorry, John, for intruding on your private matters, but Craig said it was necessary."

"Craig was absolutely right. This is no small thing. The costs are astronomical and quite selfless when you consider that those involved will never see the results."

"There are actually people who plan to put themselves in stasis for 800 years to catch the 'next bus,'" Riya explained.

I shook my head. "That takes courage. The risk is that they'll get eaten by a hungry mob or something. Eight hundred years – that's incredible. We're just going under in 200-year intervals…"

"That's the second time you've let something slip tonight – are you coming with us?" Riya asked, looking at me.

I looked into her eyes and replied, "Yes, absolutely, I'm in."

Riya squealed and hugged me tightly. "Thank you, John, thank you. I would have gone without you, of course, but I think we're such a great team… I mean, work team." Now it was my turn to laugh.

"We sure are, we sure are."

Riya continued happily, "Craig will be so relieved when he hears. He said from the start that you'd come, but I suppose I'm a skeptic to the end. What a relief – thank you, John."

"Thank you," I replied. "Now that the decision is made, I feel a huge weight lifted. I'm actually looking forward to it now. I was scheduled to go to Brussels next week for some consultations in neighboring countries. More or less hopeless projects I was supposed to inject some life into just to keep them afloat. But now we can start focusing on keeping 1,600 people alive in our new world."

"Fantastic news," Craig said, beaming like the sun. "The last piece of the puzzle is in place; you two will make an incredible team to lead the expedition."

"I have no doubt about it," I replied, looking at Riya, who smiled and looked relieved.

"Now, Riya, why don't you give John an overview of what lies ahead before departure," Craig said.

Riya spoke up, "Our next task is to select the participants. We received over 100,000 applications, which we've now narrowed down to 3,000. Two hundred specialists in various fields have already been chosen: doctors, veterinarians, engineers in construction, shipbuilding, road building, etc. Additionally, we have nurses, midwives, several energy technicians, and many others I can't recall at the moment. And of course, agronomists. Everything essential has been considered, and all specialists have some experience leading small teams and are prepared to train others. In a way, we're going back to the Stone Age, though with a fair amount of technology to start with. But all telecommunications, solar cells, etc., have a limited lifespan, so after a generation or so, we'll slide back a few centuries in Earth's technological development, so to speak. Therefore, it's vital to pass on the knowledge of technology to future generations so they can gradually redevelop it. If we don't train the next generation, we'll quickly find ourselves back in the actual Stone Age."

Craig interjected, "One thing we'd like you to think about is the political structure of the group. We don't want Viridis to end up like Earth today after 4-5,000 years."

"That was actually the first thing that came to my mind before I accepted the assignment – exactly what you mentioned. Democracy is out of the question with such a small group; it would never work and could lead to danger. Likewise, monarchy or dictatorship. Anarchism and communism have never truly been tested and have always ended as in Orwell's book, *'All animals are equal, but some animals are more equal than others.'* We still need to create a society where everyone feels valuable and contributes to the community, removing the mindset that there's a position of power. I have an idea in mind; I'll share more when it's fully formed," I concluded.

"Wonderful," said Craig, "I can see now we chose the right person with Riya to lead the project."

"Yes, plus we're working for free," I had to add. We laughed heartily, and Craig thought it was a good idea to bring out a bottle of champagne. As he filled our glasses, I added that I was very grateful WSA promised to take care of our families.

"To the greatest endeavor in modern history," Craig said, and we all joined in the toast.

I spent the night on Quasitor, as did Riya in the room next door. The rooms were quite small, like a cabin on a ship, with a bed, two chairs, a small table, and a bathroom. I understood that all rooms on Quasitor were identical. I liked the shower: "Leyla, shower at 37 degrees, warm dry," and a warm air blast dried my body. "Leyla, cool dry." It was simple and convenient – no need for a towel. I did feel like I wasn't entirely alone, though, as Leyla responded to my commands unfailingly and immediately.

"Leyla, can you see me, or can you only hear me?"

"All my knowledge and information come via your microchip. I can't actually see you, unfortunately."

"Not much to look at, I can tell you."

"Don't be so modest," replied Leyla.

I chuckled and asked, "Is Riya awake?"

"Riya is in the cafeteria. Would you like me to call her?"

"No, thanks; I'll head there myself."

Riya was deep in thought as I approached her.

"Oh, hey, I was lost in my thoughts and didn't see you coming."

"Is something bothering you?"

"Not at all," she replied. "I was mostly thinking about my family. No matter how you look at it, it's a bit melancholy."

"I understand how you feel. You haven't told me much about your family, Riya."

"A fairly typical middle-class family, I'd say. My dad is a relatively successful tailor and trained my brothers from a young age. We have about 20 branches, mostly in India but one in London. Dad would visit me there occasionally while I was studying medicine at Cambridge. My brothers are both married with typical Indian families."

"And you, have you ever considered having a family and children?"

"I had a couple of short relationships during my time at Cambridge, but I was always so focused on studying and researching that the guys lost interest – and so did I, to be honest. British pub life never interested me, so I got a reputation for being boring, which led to fewer suitors toward the end of my studies. And that suited me just fine. At the military academy in India, the men had too much respect for me, so I think no one dared approach me," Riya replied, laughing.

Damn, she's beautiful, I thought and went to get coffee.

Riya called after me, "Don't think you can get away – there's no Mrs. Carter nearby, is there?"

"A similar story to yours, except for the tailoring and medical education. Mainly work-related, always some project going on. And when you think about how short life is, it seems so pointless. My last relationship ended because we could never get our schedules to align. Sometimes we went a month without seeing each other, so we saw no reason to continue."

"Cynthia," said Riya.

"Yes," I laughed, "Cynthia."

"Sorry," Riya said, "I don't actually know much about your personal life – your mom mentioned her, that's all. That didn't sound good either."

We both laughed. "Oh, forget it, the past is long gone. Now we can look forward with speed. We're about to leap 400 years into the future."

"We need to get started on the selection of participants. I can set it up; I helped with the first rounds. Craig and I laughed until we cried at some of the applications. '*Can I share a tent with my best friend?*' '*What time is bedtime in the evenings?*' '*Do you have mosquito repellent, or should I bring my own?*'"

I threw my head back and laughed. "Good thing I avoided that part."

6. THE APPLICATIONS

Riya suggested a picnic by the beach, where we could also take a look at the applications we needed to reduce to 1,398 people. The 200 specialists were already selected, as were Riya and I.

"It's been at least 20 years since I last had a picnic – sounds great," I replied.

"I've packed some food and drinks, and I'll bring a small screen so we can go through some applications," Riya responded. "I even have a WSA cap for you; the sun's blazing."

"You seem good at this sort of thing. I'd probably end up lost and badly sunburned. It's nice having someone who thinks things through first. I tend to act first and think later," I continued.

"Don't try to fool me; I know all about your work," Riya laughed.

The silent giant acted as our driver again, taking us down to the beach. We parked outside what must have once been a beach bar or something similar. It was a bit run-down, but beautifully located, and provided shade from the scorching sun. We sat at a table.

The silent giant spoke up, "Excuse me, Mr. Carter, may I say a few words?"

"Of course, and call me John – I didn't even know you could speak."

"Thank you, si… John. Yes, I just wanted to let you know I am one of the applicants. Craig thought I'd be a good fit for the mission, but I don't want that to influence your selection of the others. Please make your own choices."

"That's news to me too," Riya replied.

"Have a seat with us," I said.

"Tell us about yourself; I'm curious," Riya added.

"My name is Mike Richter. I'm a sergeant and part of the team responsible for security on-site. I also act as Craig's bodyguard when he leaves the space center – he's a highly controversial figure these days."

"Yes, I understand that. Did you grow up in Fort Lauderdale?" I asked.

"My whole short life; I'm turning 24 soon and have lived here the entire time. We more or less lived in a slum, but we had a roof over our heads and sometimes electricity, depending on whether Mom managed to pay the bill before Dad drank away the money. Dad was an alcoholic, and as long as I can remember, he was always drunk. He was also very aggressive, and Mom and I bore the brunt of it. But I was already big as a kid, and at fourteen, I gave him a beating after he came home drunk again. After that, he didn't dare touch us anymore, instead focusing on breaking the few things we had at home. When I was 16, the hospital called to say that Dad had been in a knife fight and wouldn't make it. We arrived at his bedside just as he shouted his last words, 'It's fantastic,' and then he died. The nurse said, 'He must have been a fine man when he was alive.' I figured his last words were probably meant for his last drink. Mom replied, 'Cremate the bastard and dump his ashes in the trash.' Then she turned on her heel and left. Mom died two years later in a pandemic, but at least she found some peace before she went. After that, I made my way to Fort Moore in Georgia for basic training with the Army, and here I am. This wasn't meant to be a sob story; there are plenty more like it out there. I'm grateful for everything the Army has given me."

Riya looked at me with sadness, almost with tears in her eyes.

"Mike, how would you feel if I chose you as my and Riya's right hand on this mission? We need someone like you."

Mike lit up. "That would be amazing. Of course, I'd say yes," he replied, then became more serious. "But what would Craig think of this?"

I replied, "I don't give a damn. He chose me as the leader of the group, so he'll have to live with it," I said with a smile. "Welcome aboard."

Mike shot up and stretched his arms to the ceiling, "Thank you, John, thank you, Riya – you won't regret this!" He hugged us both at the same time, and that's when I realized just how huge he was. We all laughed and sat back down. Riya pulled out sandwiches and drinks from the basket, and we ate and chatted.

"But put on one of the applications, Riya, so we can get started," I asked Riya.

"Should I step away?" Mike asked.

"Stay; we're the Three Musketeers now," Riya laughed. "I think you could be good at this."

"Alright, let's get going. All applicants were asked to make a two-minute video about themselves. Everyone is chipped, so they've all gone through automatic health screenings, and their genes have been checked. We're really looking for subtle qualities. One thing that may sound odd in today's world is that all are heterosexual. I'm sure you understand why – we are, after all, colonizing a new planet. But ladies and playboys, here comes the first one: Trine Gudjohnsdottir from Reykjavik, Iceland."

Trine was a sporty 20-year-old who could have been a model for any women's magazine. She cheerfully concluded with, "I'm a vegetarian, but that shouldn't be a problem – there must be plenty of edible plants on Viridis."

"Well, she probably blew her application with that last sentence," Mike said. "Damn, though – I would've liked to meet her." We laughed.

"Yes, unfortunately," I said, "you must be prepared to eat whatever's available. But she was easy to reject. It'll probably get tougher from here on; we'll have to rely on instinct. You have to consider if you're willing to live with this person for the rest of your life. Let's head back to Quasitor and get started. We'll split the applications into three groups. If you're unsure, put the person in the 'maybe' pile, and we'll review those together in the end. I'll let Craig know you're officially part of our project and that your military career is over."

"This day took a turn," Mike replied. "But I'm happy, grateful, and thrilled."

Riya responded, "I think I speak for both John and me when I say the pleasure is ours. We have tons of work ahead, so you might start missing the Army soon."

"No," Mike replied. "With how things look, a lot of unpleasant things will happen soon. It feels like you've given me a lifeboat."

"I see you have a keen eye for people," Craig said. "As much as I hate to lose him, I'm glad he's getting this opportunity. He's had a tough life, and I thank you for giving him a chance – you won't find anyone more loyal!"

"Yes, both Riya and I took a liking to him. I've brought him on board to help with selecting the participants."

"That's good; delegate tasks to him – he'll execute them perfectly," I shook hands with Craig and headed to Quasitor to continue our work.

In the following days, we made significant progress with the applications. Generally, they were quite similar – most applicants were young, 18-25 years old, sporty, and of course, healthy, as revealed by the microchip screening. No one even wore glasses. It may sound extreme, as if we were seeking superhumans with exceptional genes, but that was precisely the case, whichever way you looked at it. They wanted to minimize risks. This group would be settling a new planet, and the group was incredibly small for such a task. WSA hoped that couples would form, families would start, and the gene pool would be sufficient so that within a few generations, tens of thousands of people would populate the new planet.

I started to feel old and perhaps a bit like an outsider, being the clear oldest among them. And yet, I was the one tasked with creating a baby boom – despite never having had children or even time to think about it. I think Riya was having similar thoughts, and I had certainly noticed some interest from her. The best part was that we worked together incredibly well. But she was 10 years younger, and among the specialists, there were men her age. The specialists would arrive on Quasitor 15 days before departure, just under a week from now. Together, we'd then have a couple of weeks to prepare before the participants arrived just a few days before departure.

I had previously asked what would happen if someone got "cold feet" and wanted to drop out of the project. I was told that once someone said yes, there was no turning back, and this had been thoroughly explained to the participants. In the worst case, they would be put into forced stasis, meaning they wouldn't be woken after 200 years but would remain in stasis for the full 400 years. This was to prevent potential problems upon awakening. The risk of not waking up after 400 years in stasis was significantly higher than with two 200-year periods. It was estimated that the chance of not waking increased from one per thousand to around five percent. So I didn't think we'd have any issues in that regard.

Time passed, and Christmas was approaching. Riya was planning a trip to India to say goodbye to her family, while I was heading to New Jersey to do the same and to celebrate Christmas with my family one last time.

"Mike, would you like to come to my parents' home for Christmas?" It was a spontaneous invitation, but I knew he didn't have any family left.

"Thank you, boss, for the invitation, but I think it's best you spend your farewell with your loved ones without me. I'd just be in the way."

"Nonsense," I replied. "Mom would be overjoyed to take care of you. And besides, there's always too much food on the table, so this way, we can avoid waste."

"Well, when you put it that way, I'd be happy to come. I've never really experienced Christmas – celebrations on the base were mostly just eating and drinking. And since I swore off alcohol after seeing what it did to my father, I always left when things got out of hand."

"Perfect," I said. "I'll let Mom know; she'll be thrilled."

7. CHRISTMAS

Christmas was exactly as I had imagined it – too much food, doting attention from Mom, especially toward Mike, whom she immediately adored. She constantly brought out chocolates and treats in an endless stream, to the point where I had to ask if she was trying to give us diabetes before departure. Mike, however, was thrilled and never said no, savoring the attention he'd never experienced before.

I was generous with gifts: Dad got the leaf blower he'd been missing from his already well-stocked garden shed, and Mom got a new dishwasher, which Mike and I managed to install, not to mention the Santa with the sleigh that I'd bought in Helsinki. For Mike, Riya and I had jointly purchased a hunting knife with a sheath and a sharpening stone. We had engraved it with the words, *To our friend Mike, Christmas 2173 – John & Riya*. Mike stared at it, teary-eyed. "This is the nicest thing anyone's ever given me. Thank you. I'll keep it with me always."

I told my parents that I had transferred all my savings to their account and that they could live in comfort if they wished. They would also receive my monthly ICPA salary. As I put it, "Where I'm going, money won't matter." It felt like a huge release; it must be how Buddhist monks feel – free from the pressures of the capitalist world.

The evening before my departure to Fort Lauderdale, I got a call from Riya.

"Hey, how has the Christmas celebration been?"

"Thanks for asking; I feel like an overfed chicken. Mike, on the other hand, seems to have a bottomless stomach. And you?"

"Well, we don't celebrate Christmas in our circles. We have different ideas about how ascension should go compared to you Christians," she laughed.

"Well, at least I know my ascension begins in three weeks. We're heading to the space center tomorrow – when will you arrive?"

"Same here; I'll be there by tomorrow afternoon. And one more thing… I miss you."

I swallowed and replied, "I miss you too."

"Can we talk about it tomorrow?" she asked a little uncertainly.

"Absolutely, we will. Goodnight."

"Goodnight, John."

Our goodbye was bittersweet, with many tears on both sides. Dad tried to hold back his tears but couldn't quite manage. His final words were, "I'm incredibly proud of you, but it feels so hard. Don't feel guilty, though; you've made sure we're set for life. What more can a parent ask from their son?" Mom mostly cried and wished me luck. From the door, she shouted, "Mike, take care of my son!" Mike replied, "You have nothing to worry about when he's with me."

We stepped into the small electric helicopter WSA insisted we use, as the risks on the streets outside monitored areas had become too great.

8. RIYA

As soon as we arrived at Quasitor, I headed straight to my room, feeling bittersweet but also relieved to have said goodbye to Mom and Dad. It had been nagging at the back of my mind for a long time. I lay on the bed for a moment, gathering my thoughts. I wondered if Riya had already arrived, so I decided to take a shower and ask Leyla afterward.

"Leyla, can you play something classical from my list?" I asked her. Leyla chose Motörhead's "Ace of Spades." "Don't forget the joker," I sang along in the shower. After I finished, I asked Leyla, "Has Riya arrived?" "Yes, she's in the cafeteria. Should I call her?" I simply replied, "No, thanks." I felt nervous – incredibly nervous. I didn't know how Riya felt about me. *Damn it,* I felt like an insecure 15-year-old, worrying whether the pimple on my nose was shining like a beacon in the dim light of the school dance. The pimple was gone now, so I had to go see what the verdict was.

Riya was sitting with her back to me when I approached, talking to Mike. I was just a few meters away from their table when she noticed me and came over. She hugged me tightly, and then I honestly don't know what happened, but after a moment, we kissed each other fiercely and passionately. I felt tears streaming down my cheeks; I wasn't sure if they were hers or mine – probably both.

"Wow, wow, wow! If I can't be the best man at the wedding, I'll be very disappointed," Mike laughed. Then we all laughed, both from hysteria and relief that this part was over. "What just happened?" I wondered, laughing happily while holding Riya's hand.

"I've felt this way for a while but didn't know how to act. It's nice that it came so spontaneously," Riya laughed.

"I agree; this isn't exactly my area of expertise, but I'm happy," I replied.

"I could see it coming, but for once, I thought it best not to interfere," Mike chuckled.

We ordered food from the robot cart and shared stories about our Christmases and farewells with our families. Mike shared that it was an amazing experience to celebrate Christmas with a normal family. "I hope to have my own family to celebrate Christmas with too."

"Family life is something we all dream of, and I've heard the dating scene looks pretty bright for the future. That's why I have to secure the best before the beauties arrive," Riya laughed.

"I believe luck is on my side," I added. "We have exciting times ahead; I wonder what the beginning will look like."

"A windbreak with an outdoor toilet will suffice for me at first, as long as I have you with me – not in the toilet, of course," Riya laughed.

"Well, we'll have to push the engineers to get something set up for us. Only the best will do for Viridis' princess," Mike suggested.

"Good thinking there," I chimed in.

We spent a few more hours chatting and planning for the specialists' arrival. Soon, there would be 200 more people here. But right now, Riya was the focal point of my life; I was in love – perhaps for the first time – and it felt incredible. And after this day, we would be living in the same room.

9. THE SPECIALISTS

I woke up a few minutes before Leyla was supposed to wake us. I looked at Riya as she slept, her long black hair contrasting beautifully against the white sheets. I kissed her on the back, and she turned over, smiling.

"Good morning, you're already awake."

"I wanted to take a minute to look at you. Did you sleep well? I mean, it's not the world's widest bed."

"I slept happily and well. If it was too cramped, you could try Mike's bed," she laughed.

"I think Mike has a hard enough time fitting alone in his own bed, so I'll settle for you," I replied.

"You'll have me, and for a long time. But we only have one bathroom, so I'll go to my room and shower there, and we'll meet in the cafeteria – we have a lot to plan."

"Yes, my dear, see you there."

"Play something classical," I asked Leyla as I stood in the shower. I laughed as Leyla played "It's So Easy to Fall in Love" by Linda Ronstadt. I started to suspect she wasn't entirely honest when she said she could only sense us through the microchip. She clearly knew we were together through it but would probably blush if she actually saw what we were doing. Not a great time to get paranoid.

"Thanks for the music, Leyla. What made you choose that?"

Leyla replied, "I'm programmed to pick up on certain emotions, but don't worry, I still can't see you." *Is she reading my mind too?* Time for coffee before I lose it.

Mike was already there, and I knew from experience that it took much longer for the ladies to get ready. I grabbed my coffee and sat with Mike.

"Well?" Mike said.

"Oh, shut up," I laughed.

"Show me the list of specialists again," Mike pulled it out of his briefcase.

"Thanks," I said, scanning it. "We'll wait for Riya to split it into two groups."

"Two? Why?" Mike asked.

"We'll wait for Riya. I've learned that whether you're explaining something to two or a hundred people, it's easier to do it once for everyone. Saves both time and patience."

"Maybe you should have joined the Army; that's straight out of the textbook," Mike laughed heartily.

"I'm too much of a pacifist for that," I replied.

Riya joined us at the table, looking like she was ready for a gala dinner. I raised a finger toward Mike.

"Good morning is enough, thank you."

"Good morning," Riya said. "I see you have the lists out. I'll grab a coffee, and we'll get started if breakfast can wait a bit."

"I've already had breakfast," Mike replied.

"Oh, that surprises me," I joked.

We bantered back and forth for a while until I began.

"We'll divide them into two groups of 800 and station them a few hundred kilometers apart." Mike and Riya looked at me in surprise. "Stay calm; you'll have time to ask questions soon," I continued. "We're doing this to minimize risks. We'll build two communities. We have no idea what awaits us – what if there's an earthquake, a tsunami, or a massive swarm of poisonous wasps we didn't account for? Hell, there might even be a Tyrannosaurus Rex lurking. We have no idea what it's like there beyond the fact that it's supposed to be green and pleasant. The scans indicate that the air and gravity are similar to Earth's, the day is a bit longer, and the planet is a little larger."

Mike raised a finger.

"Go ahead," I said.

"I was just thinking about us in that division. Otherwise, the reasoning seems sound. Are any of us three going to be split up?" Mike looked concerned.

"The three of us stick together – I promise. We'll be the core of Group One, and we'll divide the specialists equally based on expertise. Both groups should be equally strong, and we'll select three leaders for each group once we get to know everyone a bit."

Mike beamed, "Yes, the Three Musketeers!"

"The *Three Musketeers*," Riya seid, laughing.

"I think," Riya said, "that we should wait to divide the groups until we see how people interact and who gets along with whom."

"You're right; for now, we'll just split them by their area of expertise," I replied.

"So, per group: 6 doctors, 6 trained medical staff, 32 builders, 4 veterinarians, 4 shipbuilders, 6 road engineers, 6 energy specialists, 18 agronomists, 6 teachers, 4 fishers, and 8 hunters."

"Where do we fit in?" Mike asked.

"If I counted correctly, that gives each group 100 specialists plus the three of us. That makes 700 participants per group."

"Good question, Mike. As I see it, we're participants. This 'king, queen, prince' arrangement will end as soon as we reach Viridis. Sure, we'll likely have some initial authority, and people will look to us at first, but that can't be the future."

"But now I'm hungry – let's eat, and then I'll tell you a bit about my political ideas. Riya already knows a little about them."

"Yeah, I'm feeling hungry too," Mike said.

"It's been half an hour since you last ate, after all," Riya laughed.

We continued after a light breakfast. "Yes, I vaguely mentioned to Craig earlier that we need a functioning political system. It almost makes me sick to use the word 'politics' these days. The democratic process has completely derailed, and people have lost all faith in politicians. The people – well, mostly the elite, those with chips – have divided themselves into different camps. Those who are starving couldn't care less about whose turn it is to sit on the liar's bench. This is already visible in the voter turnout, which is nowhere near what it was 100 years ago or more. Most people in, for example, the U.S. don't even have voting rights in that country, so how can it function when the majority can't decide anything? Well, we don't have those problems yet. But in a small group, problems can become dangerous too. Imagine if we had to vote on where to build a hospital, and the vote ended 410-390. Clearly, morale would drop for those 390 expected to help with the project. A dictatorship is out of the question as well – same issue, it divides people. No, I envision something as simple as a village committee: 20 people serving a week at a time, maybe with 2-3 meetings as needed. They'd elect a 'village elder' each week, which could be the same person if they think they're suitable. For major decisions, they could call in specialists to share their insights. Take, for example, building a hospital again. I'd think a civil engineer should decide where it's best located in terms of access, drainage, etc., rather than someone whose interest is in dog training or Thai cuisine. Simple enough – why complicate things?"

"Thoughts?" Riya sat next to me, hugging my arm, which I took as a sign she liked the idea.

"Mike?" I asked.

"I like the idea, and it's good that 'power' rotates. Everyone will feel involved, at least once a year. But one thing that worries me a bit is the weapons. We'll have some with us for hunting and such."

"You're right, Mike, and that worries me too. I haven't fully thought it through. We can talk with the hunters to get their input. And we don't even know if there's anything to hunt at all."

"Except for T-Rex, of course," Riya laughed.

"I can handle him with my new hunting knife," Mike assured.

"Let's take a break," I said.

"Oh, so that's what a break is called these days," Mike laughed.

We had two space shuttles with us on Quasitor, one as a backup. But I had already informed Craig and the management that we'd be using both. One shuttle was designed to hold 1,600 people, plus everything we'd need. By using both, we could properly stock up our supplies. They were built to land vertically once, after which they'd be permanently stationed. I intended for them to serve as a hospital and temporary shelter if needed. There was some fuss and meetings about it, but Craig eventually gave us the green light for the plan.

I asked Mike to take over and show us what was in Leyla's storage. "Yes, all of this is calculated to fit within one shuttle," Mike gestured forward. I was stunned – tons of tools, provisions, medicines, clothes, and so on. I started to realize the sheer scale of what 1,600 people would need. Riya immediately headed to the medicine area, "This is better equipped than many hospitals I've worked in. We'll have the ability to do X-rays, surgeries, we have a lab – everything. And the medicine supply is well-stocked too; we should be in good shape for the foreseeable future."

We moved on. "Mike, show me the weapons," I asked. Riya knew a lot about weapons, while I was a complete novice.

"We have 12 machine guns, the latest from the U.S. Army," Mike began.

Riya already had one in her hands, performing loading maneuvers and aiming randomly.

"Good stuff," she remarked.

"Who am I even with?" I laughed.

"These would only be for self-defense if we encounter something unknown," Mike reassured.

"As far as I'm concerned, everything is unknown until we know more about it," I replied.

"We also have four laser pistols powered by solar cells. We have enough ammunition for the machine guns for a small war. The machine guns are all equipped with scopes, so a hunter would have no problem taking down a deer from 500 meters and beyond if necessary," Mike explained.

"Well, we're not planning any wars, so that's six guns and two laser pistols per group. We're not getting any more weapons," I concluded.

The agronomists were also well-provided for – we even had a tractor with a digging scoop, which would be invaluable. We'd need to get another one for the second group. There were plenty of spare parts as well, though their lifespan wouldn't be endless. Naturally, it was electric-powered. Then there were quantities of hoes, shovels, measuring tools, and so on. Fishing gear covered everything from sharks to minnows, with nets, rods, hooks – everything was thought out.

"The specialists should check their equipment because now that we're using two shuttles, we can stock up. Craig will have to stretch the budget a bit. It's small potatoes in the grand scheme of things. Thanks for the tour, Mike. I see everything is thoroughly planned."

"I'm very pleased with it all. We're going to have a head start in the Stone Age – we'll skip thousands of years compared to what our ancestors faced," said Riya.

I continued, "We have a couple of days to plan and finetune, then the specialists and participants arrive, and soon after, we'll be on our way. It's incredible that in just three weeks, we'll be on our way."

We were starting to feel the pressure as departure approached – there was so much to organize, and the days were long. But we were becoming a well-oiled trio, each of us knowing where help was needed most and stepping in immediately. Craig was bustling around as well, giving orders left and right. He had been part of the Quasitor project from the beginning, for decades, and had led it for the past five years. This was a billion-dollar project, and if it failed, space exploration would take many steps backward. Everything was planned down to the last detail: the journey to the moon base and then shuttle transfers to Quasitor. I began to realize the enormity of my own role – I almost felt like Moses must have in the wilderness. But everything looked good, and we ran around in what seemed like organized chaos, more nerves than real problems. Granted, my decision to bring both shuttles to Viridis had made things more rushed. But believe it or not, there was a backup plan for that too.

Tomorrow, the specialists would arrive, and we'd have a welcoming lunch and other events to get to know them. The final step would be the arrival of the remaining participants. All would be accommodated on the Quasitor replica, but everything was ready for it. We also had 40 reserve participants living in the area. However, they wouldn't board Quasitor unless someone fell seriously ill.

Riya and I didn't have much time for each other, but we comforted ourselves with the thought that things would calm down once we arrived. But how calm could it be, really? We'd need to set up housing for everyone and ensure that everyone found their place in the new society. I trusted that the specialists, and surely the participants too, would contribute a lot. After all, we were all in the same boat, each of us seeking happiness – something that had become difficult to find on Earth lately.

The press was also on-site but was not allowed to publish anything until Quasitor3 was well underway. This was to prevent riots or sabotage attempts against the project. These were exciting times, and it showed in everyone. Mike was incredible – an excellent organizer and a calming presence for everyone, always with a twinkle in his eye and something funny to say. Riya was busy organizing and cataloging the medical supplies and equipment. As my mom had said, "a fantastic person." I'd also gotten used to Leyla and realized how much time we saved by using her amazing capabilities.

"Leyla, what is Riya doing?"

"She's packing the ultrasound machine. At her current pace, it should be done in three minutes and thirty seconds."

"Could you ask her to join me for a lunch break when she's finished?"

"Will do, John."

And that's how it went – I'd surely miss her, though I guessed Linda would be just as sharp.

10. SAY YES

After lunch, Leyla informed me that I was to meet Craig in his office.

"Just me?" I asked.

"Mr. Thomas didn't specify otherwise," Leyla replied. I shrugged and looked at Riya. "See you soon," I said, giving her a quick kiss before heading off.

"Thanks for coming, John. Have a seat," Craig said.

"To what do I owe the honor?" I wondered, especially as Mike was already there. Craig began,

"Well, you've certainly made us earn our salaries with your changes. Not that I mind – this is why you're leading the group, and all the changes have been for the better. But…" Craig stared straight at me, "Not everything is perfect; not everything is as it should be."

"Sorry, I'm not quite following…" I began, but Craig raised his hand, signaling me to "shut up and listen." So I listened.

"I understand you're in a relationship with Riya Mendis," he said.

"Yes, that's true," I started. "But I can assure you that all the changes have come from me, so she – "

The "shut up" hand came up again, and Craig continued, "You're getting married today, and then it'll be perfect," he laughed.

"What?" was all I managed to say, as eloquent as always.

"I've thought this through and planned it with Mike."

I looked at Mike, whose grin looked like it might split his head in two.

"Sorry, boss."

"Do you love her?" Craig asked.

"With all my heart, but we've only known each other a few days."

"Then it's settled. Tonight, in front of all the specialists and a good number of the staff, you'll propose."

"But what the hell happens if she says no?"

"In front of all those people and your parents?" Craig replied.

"Our parents? What do you mean?"

"They're on their way here and will arrive just in time for the proposal." Craig and Mike laughed, exchanging glances.

"And Riya doesn't know about the proposal or that her parents are coming?" I asked.

"Not a clue," Mike chimed in. "And Leyla has been briefed to ensure you don't let anything slip."

I ruffled my hair, "I don't think I've ever been this nervous in my life. Riya is bound to pick up on this."

"Well, time to bring out your acting skills, John. It'll be fine, you'll see."

"What was that about?" Riya asked when I returned.

"It was about the tractor." Oh, I was a real actor – a complete fool.

"The tractor?" Riya laughed.

"Yes, the other one we're bringing with the digging scoop. Craig had a picture and asked if it looked okay."

"Strange," Riya said. "I didn't know you knew about that stuff."

"Me? I can't even drive a car. I told him to leave it to the construction team tomorrow," I continued to lie. I needed a quick change of subject.

"I was thinking of jogging down to the beach – just a few kilometers. Want to join?" I almost hoped she'd say no so I wouldn't have to spout more nonsense.

"Of course, I'll come. Should we wear swimsuits underneath so we can take a dip?"

"Perfect," I replied. We jogged at an easy pace to the beach, undressed, and ran into the water. It had been years since I'd swum in the ocean; it was usually hotel pools or my condo pool. It felt amazing. I held Riya in my arms, looked into her eyes, and said, "Thank you for being here." We kissed and walked hand-in-hand back to shore.

We went to our rooms, and after a shower, we started preparing for the specialists' arrival.

They arrived in a convoy of buses. We met them in the WSA cafeteria, the largest space available, where we'd be mingling this evening to get to know them better. Craig welcomed everyone, and Riya and I said a few words, expressing our hopes that everyone was excited to take part in the world's greatest adventure. We told them that we'd all be moving to Quasitor for an hour's rest and a chance to shower if they wanted. Then, Mike and a few staff members would give them a tour to show them what the next 400 years might look like. We'd reconvene here at 6 for dinner and socializing. Everyone applauded, clearly eager for the day's program. Their adventure was beginning now. But of all the people in the room, I was definitely the most nervous. Craig gave me a reassuring wink, but it didn't help much. My head spun with thoughts: what if she said no? I'd be seeing my parents again, even though we'd already had a tearful goodbye. I knew my mom would be overjoyed, and my proposal would be the icing on the cake. Oh boy… it didn't help when Riya said, "Look, a band is setting up – apparently there'll be music too."

"Yes, we can even cut a rug," I joked nervously.

"I think I'll go take a nap in our room and skip the tour. Will you come with me?"

"I'll come in a bit; you go ahead. I'll try not to wake you."

"I don't mind if you wake me," Riya replied with a wink and a laugh. *Good grief, is everyone winking today?*

Once Riya left, I sat down at a table. Craig joined me.

"How are you feeling, John?" he asked.

"On a scale of going to an unknown planet 400 years away or proposing, the proposal wins hands down. I've never been this scared in my life."

"It'll go fine, you'll see," Craig reassured me. "By the way, here's a ring. Leyla measured Riya, so it should fit perfectly." He handed me a silk box. Inside was a gold ring with a red ruby.

"Wow, it's beautiful. Thanks, Craig."

"That's not all. This is the engagement ring for the proposal, and you'll get married right afterward. Mike will be your best man – he insisted. There'll be another ring for Riya and one for you."

"Craig, are you married?"

"Yes, we got married on the moon. That's actually where I got the idea," Craig laughed. "We got engaged in the rocket on the way to the moon."

I went to our room and lay down beside Riya, careful not to wake her. Leyla woke us up an hour before the gathering.

"You didn't wake me," Riya smiled.

"No, I thought I'd let you recharge for the evening," I smiled back.

"I'll take a shower and get ready."

"I'll do the same, though with a bit less prep. I'll come by when I'm ready."

Half an hour later, I was ready, wearing a polo shirt with a jacket. Riya looked stunning in a deep red dress with black heels. Her makeup was perfect, and her black hair gleamed with a hint of blue.

"Leyla, play Eric Clapton's 'You Look Wonderful Tonight,'" I asked.

"May I have this dance, my dear?"

We swayed to the music in the small room.

"What's this beautiful song?" Riya asked.

"A little hobby of mine – I love classical music from 150-200 years ago. And this one feels right for the moment."

"Thank you, John. I think I'm the happiest person on Earth – and Viridis," she said.

"You're the second happiest," I replied, kissing her. "But we should go. People probably have a lot of questions; I'm looking forward to the evening. And one more thing – you look stunning."

We stood with Craig before the assembled specialists and many WSA staff. Craig introduced himself and me as the leader of the expedition and wished everyone a pleasant evening with great food, music, and, most importantly, a chance to get to know each other. Tomorrow, we'd delve more into our future plans, but tonight was just for enjoyment. Lots of smiles and applause followed, and then Craig handed me the microphone.

"Hi, as Craig said, my name's John – no Mr. or Sir before it, just John for all of us. And I'd like to introduce one more person. Riya, would you come up here?" Riya pointed at herself. "Yes, come on up, don't be shy," I said, as a few people whistled at her.

"Riya will be my right hand on this journey, and in this moment, I thought it fitting to ask for her left one too." I knelt before her, my voice trembling.

"Riya," I said, "I haven't known you long, but I want you by my side for whatever time we have left – 500 years or so. Riya, would you make me the happiest person in the universe? Will you marry me?"

"Yes," Riya said, tearfully. I slid the ruby ring onto her finger. "She said yes." Everyone cheered, and many tears were shed as well.

"Riya, turn around," I said. Riya's parents came running up, and a round of hugs began. My mom and dad came up, both crying – Dad couldn't even try to hide his tears

Craig took the microphone. "Allow me to congratulate you both on your engagement, on behalf of myself and WSA. But Riya, Riya, don't think the surprises end here. I love you like the daughter I never had, so only the best for you – now you're getting married." The crowd's cheers grew louder. Riya couldn't speak; she just cried, hugging me, my parents, and her own parents. I felt it deeply – she was happy, and I was happy. This engagement and wedding would be talked about for decades on Viridis. Craig continued, "As the representative of Viridis, I will officiate your wedding. Come and stand on either side of me." The ceremony was short and straightforward, with Mike proudly handling the rings, his wide smile never faltering.

I took the microphone. "Apologies for our little surprise show. Thanks to all of you for putting up with it." Laughter and applause filled the room. "But tonight is for you and all of us, so let's avoid more speeches. Now it's your turn. And if anyone else wants to get married, the opportunity's here now that we're on a roll. Thank you, everyone." A table was set for our families, along with Craig and Mike. I looked at Riya, "Sorry, Mrs. Carter, but the masterminds behind the scheme were actually these two," I said, gesturing toward Craig and Mike.

"So you thought," Riya said, winking at Mike.

I gaped at them in turn. "Darn, fooled again," I laughed, and we shared a good laugh together.

"In any case, I'm overjoyed," my mom chimed in, and everyone agreed, toasting to that.

It was now clear where the acting talent in the Carter family lay. Everyone laughed with me at myself. "What if she says no?" "It was about the tractor," and so on. It even turned out that my parents were in on the "scheme." Craig said, "The only real suspense was if you'd go along with it when we talked in my office. After that, we just had to keep up the charade." We toasted again, and I thanked all the plotters for what they'd done. "I have no experience with things like this, so it might've taken me a while to act on my own."

"No need," Riya said, "I would have done it myself if it took too long." She was wonderful – my wife. It was a different kind of mingling than we'd initially planned, but all the specialists came by to congratulate us, giving us a good sense of the group.

We all wore badges with our titles and names. Riya's read "Riya Carter, Consultant Dr., and First Lieutenant." Clearly, everyone was confident about the outcome, as the badge even had my last name on it. But I was the one who proposed, and she knew it, so what could have gone wrong? She wasn't wearing the badge when I proposed, though. Mine read "Project Leader John Carter," an odd title considering the project had been ongoing for decades, and I'd only been involved for a few weeks.

The rest of the evening passed peacefully. The orchestra played dance music, and Riya and I took the floor for the obligatory "wedding waltz." I also shared a dance with my overjoyed mom. Riya danced with my dad and her own father as well. A giant cake was rolled out too – a fairly typical wedding in all respects. Craig came over to tell us that we had a villa reserved just for us for the night. Our parents would stay in the villa next door, giving us time to say goodbye again in the morning. We slipped away quietly, as we'd be working with the specialists tomorrow morning at nine. I noted with pleasure that the punch consumption was very moderate.

We got into the self-driving car that took us to "our" villa for our wedding night. "Thank you, Riya. I want you to know that this is big, very big, for me. I promise I'll do everything to make you happy."

"And I promise you exactly the same," she replied with tears in her eyes.

After our wedding night, we shared a farewell breakfast, and then my parents left by private electric helicopter to New Jersey, giving the neighbors something to gossip about. Riya's parents were escorted to a private electric plane – WSA was generous.

Riya turned to me. "As much as I'd love to stay in the villa, we have a lot to do. Time to roll up our sleeves and get started."

"Yes, ma'am, Mrs. Carter. I hear you. And we need to find a suitable trio to lead Group Two."

11. THE TRIO

We gathered in Quasitor's cafeteria and, seeing that breakfast was over, I asked for everyone's attention. "Thank you all for last night; it was great to see everyone could join, not that you had much choice," I joked, earning some laughter. "We have a lot of work ahead. Time is flying, and soon we'll have the rest of the participants here, and then, we're off on a little trip. Riya has divided you into your respective fields of expertise so you can start planning for the future." I went on to explain the division into two groups and briefly outlined my political idea. Well, it wasn't an idea anymore – this was how it would be. I couldn't give them the option to oppose the politics; otherwise, we'd soon have full democracy and the chaos that comes with it.

We agreed that Riya, Mike, and I wouldn't mention yet that we were looking for leaders for Group Two. We'd stay observant and see how the day unfolded. Riya took charge of the group with the doctors, veterinarians, and teachers – a total of 44 people. I took the largest group, and we decided to use the WSA cafeteria for maximum space. This group consisted of house builders, road builders, and energy specialists, totaling 88 people. Mike led the group of boat builders, fishers, hunters, and, perhaps the most critical, the agronomists. The agronomists were responsible for ensuring a stable food supply. We had seeds for all the common grains, as well as corn and rice. They would naturally work closely with the road builders later on. For now, though, this was the structure we thought best. Mike had 68 people in his group and immediately took firm command, leading them off to a larger room set aside for group work.

We also had pigs, sows specifically – 100 of them, which the veterinarians would artificially inseminate. They were already sedated on Quasitor 3 and would remain so throughout the 400-year journey. It was expected that 10-15% of the animals might not survive the trip, but there would still be plenty. A sow produces between 8-14 piglets and has a gestation period of about 115 days. If we didn't slaughter them within the first two years, we'd soon have plenty of them. The veterinarians' task would be to ensure good genetic diversity, avoid inbreeding, handle vaccinations, and much more. They'd work closely with the agronomists and house builders. Additionally, we had 2,000 fertilized chicken eggs. So, there would be plenty of work for everyone once we arrived. That's why it was essential to get effective teams established among the specialists. Naturally, all participants would be allowed to help as well. No one would be forced to, but we strongly believed everyone would want to contribute. I hoped that within six months, we'd have a reasonably functioning society, with everyone under a roof, and hopefully, many would have found a partner. Riya and I had certainly set a good example, I thought with a smile.

We made significant progress in just a few hours. I was especially impressed by a guy from Peru, Jose Borgas. He'd already done his homework and presented his vision of what the village could look like. He projected his ideas from his computer onto a screen, which Leyla helped display. The village he envisioned was almost idyllic. He had adjusted it since hearing we'd be split into two groups, but the houses made of clay and stone, with roads between the 400 homes, a water purification plant, running water, well systems, and even geothermal heating possibilities – he had thought of everything. He received applause and sat down.

I spoke up, "Very good, Jose, thank you. What do the rest of you think? Can we use this as a foundation to work from? Your expertise is welcome, so let's divide into groups and develop this idea. You all know something useful, so share your knowledge and build on what we have. And also consider agriculture, especially the pigsty – no one will want to live too close to it. We'll get manure from that and the chicken coops, so plan where it would be most efficient to place them. You'll also need to include a school for future needs, as well as for training within your fields of expertise. We'll be miles ahead of our ancestors as long as we pass on what we know. Damn, this is fun – we're building an ideal world. I'm going to make the rounds and check on the other groups. Take lunch whenever you feel like it."

I wanted to go back to Quasitor and meet Riya. To be honest, I was already missing her a little after two hours. Was this how it would feel from now on? I hoped so. Riya had already gotten her group work started, so I didn't want to interfere since I didn't understand much – or really anything at all. Riya came over and asked if everything was going well, and we sat down a bit away from the others. "Yes, actually. It's reassuring to know we have people we can rely on. And here?"

"Everything's great. They're even more skilled and experienced than I expected," she replied. "The teachers might feel a bit out of place, though – it's not exactly their field," she added.

"I can borrow them for a while. We're planning a school, and they'll definitely want to give their input. Grown-up education will be the main focus at first, but eventually, there will be swings and sandboxes to consider too."

"I want little Lisa to have a red backpack," Riya joked, "but later on – no one can be pregnant during cryosleep. It could have fatal consequences."

I laughed. "And Pelle will have a blue one."

"I love you," Riya whispered and gave me a discreet kiss on the cheek.

"And how's Mike?" Riya asked.

"I'm going there now. Good luck here, and I think I might have found a leader – keep your eyes open for one too." I called over to the teachers, asking them to follow me.

"Hey, teachers," I greeted as we walked toward the room where Mike was. "I thought I'd rescue you from the boredom here. You go to the doctor when you're sick, not when you're healthy," I joked. "Today, you'll act as observers. After Mike's group, we'll go to WSA, where you can give some thoughts on where and how to build the school." They seemed relieved and happy to escape the medical discussions with Riya's group.

Mike's group was also working hard, divided by expertise. The boat builders were sketching out various types of boats, with sails and without, in different sizes. Hopefully, the right types of wood and materials would be available. It was a similar story with the hunters – we had no idea what animals, if any, would be there besides the pigs and chickens, so they would need to be versatile. The same went for the fishers. The agronomists, however, were already enthusiastically mapping out fields, irrigation systems, and more. I asked Leyla to display Jose's ideal village on the screen, which was met with approving whistles and prompted even more discussion. The teachers fit in well with the group.

"I pulled Mike aside and asked, "How's it going?"

"Great, actually! They're a fantastic bunch."

"Have you found someone?" I asked.

"Yeah, that big guy, a hunter, really funny, and seems to know a bit about everything."

"Good. Keep an eye out for anyone else, and we'll discuss it with our trio later."

"I'm taking the teachers to WSA now. See you later. Great work!"

"Thanks, boss."

"Hmph," I replied.

We arrived at the WSA cafeteria and started with lunch, which everyone else had already helped themselves to. I sat with Jose, who was already deep in lively discussions with others at the table.

"How's it going here?" I asked.

"We're all eager to arrive and get started," replied a woman with a nametag that read Ashante Otieno.

"I like the idea of clay houses. I'm from Kenya, and they're common there."

"Okay, great! Good to have expertise on that too."

"What about mortar and such?" I asked.

"I can take on that part," replied a blond guy named James Barnaby from Wales. "You mainly need sand, water, and a certain type of mineral stone, so we'll see what's available in the terrain that we can use."

"Wonderful to hear. As long as you can set up the framework, I think we'll get everything settled quickly. At first, we might need temporary shelters, like windbreaks and similar structures – the hunters probably know a lot about that, so we can consult them. To some extent, we can also live in the shuttle, which is intended to serve as a hospital initially. And don't worry, we'll have 700 participants to help as well, so you won't have to do everything alone; everyone will pitch in. We'll work on what we can for the next few days, and when the participants arrive, they'll be able to choose which group they'd like to join. We'll also need to split you into two groups, so you can indicate if there's anyone you'd prefer to work with. But remember the most important thing: 400 men and 400 women per group. It's more important than it sounds. I'm sure you understand why."

The whole day went well – much better than I expected. Everyone understood the purpose of the project, and everyone was up to the task. I thought of my ICPA projects that were stuck in bureaucracy. Everything here was so refreshingly simple: if you didn't know something, you asked the person next to you, got an answer, and moved on. I tried to be very careful not to get into technical questions; I'd only make a fool of myself. My main job was to hold the overall vision together. I had Riya and Mike, but it was just as important to find a dynamic leadership for Group Two so they wouldn't feel like the B team. I still had Jose as my candidate, but we would discuss it tonight with Riya and Mike, and if they had good candidates, we'd interview them.

We kept at it well into the evening before I called it a day. "Alright, everyone, that's enough for today. Fantastic job, but let's pace ourselves. Otherwise, it'll start to feel like work. And remember, you're not getting paid for this. Enjoy the evening, relax, and get to know each other. We'll continue tomorrow."

12 WHEN THE SHIT HIT THE FAN

We decided to have a quick meeting in our room after the day's events. It had been a perfect day in my view. I never imagined, even in my wildest dreams, how amazing and skilled the people we had with us would be. Everything looked promising. I sat on the bed, and Mike and Riya each took a chair at the small table. We had barely been seated for a minute when Leyla interrupted. "John, Riya, and Mike, you are to go to Craig's office at WSA immediately. The car is waiting outside."

"Did he mean immediately-immediately, or can we go in an hour? We were just planning to discuss some things here."

"Immediately," Leyla replied.

"Maybe Mike's getting married today," Riya said. Laughing, we got up and went to the car.

We were escorted to the meeting room where I'd first met Craig, with the large table. This time, the table was full except for six seats reserved for us. Around the walls, chairs were lined up, so I guessed there were about a hundred people in the room. Craig began without any greetings, "Have you found the three leaders for Group Two?" Straight to the point. I began to suspect something had happened but waited for an explanation.

I started, "Yes, we were about to discuss it just as we were called here."

"You must have some names," Craig said. I was starting to get a little annoyed by the pushy tone, but I could see that Craig was highly stressed.

"Yes, I was thinking of Jose Borgas."

"And Riya?"

"Yong Kodcharen, a doctor from Thailand," Riya replied.

"Mike?"

"Sakari Littlehorse from Alaska," he answered.

"Leyla, make sure Jose Borgas, Yong Kodcharen, and Sakari Littlehorse are here in five minutes. You can all take a short break; we'll continue when everyone is here."

We went over to the water dispenser. Riya clung to my arm, "What's going on?" she wondered.

Mike responded, "Something has happened, something big. I've never seen him this tense."

"We'll find out soon enough. No point in speculating, but yeah, I'm feeling uneasy too. For the first time in this project, it feels really uncomfortable," I replied.

A few minutes later, Jose, Sakari, and Yong came in, looking completely bewildered. Jose looked at me, shrugged, and held his arms out to me. "I don't know," I mouthed back. I gestured for everyone to head inside and sit down. I looked around the room, and I didn't see a single happy face; most people looked worried, and I wondered how much they knew. We took our six seats. Craig began, "Jose Borgas, you have been chosen as the leader of Group Two;

Yong Kodcharen will be your second-in-command, and Sakari Littlehorse will be your deputy. Do you accept these roles?" They all nodded quietly. "Then, let's get down to business. Leyla, put the bulletin up on the screen."

John Carter is to lead 1,600 people to a foreign planet. Each participant is valued at over a billion dollars. They will live in luxury while the world starves. Craig Thomas has refused to comment on the reports. UPA (United People's Army) will stop the upcoming launch. If you have military training, contact your local UPA office; people with medical knowledge are also needed because blood is going to flow. We will take control of the world and make it a place where we all can live. Power to the people!

At the end, there was an image of Craig and me hanging from a lamppost. It didn't affect me much; I was used to death threats from my work with ICPA. But I saw it had shaken Riya. She clung to my arm and rested her head on my chest. Craig spoke, "We've been threatened before, but not on this scale. General Johnson, could you give us an overview of the situation?"

"For starters, we don't know who leaked the news to UPA, and it's irrelevant at this point. We have extended the security zone by an additional 20 km radius. We are at Risk Level 1, equivalent to a war situation. We are relatively safe for now, and the risk of missile attacks is low. But you'll likely hear gunfire if you move outside Quasitor's replica. Stay in Quasitor; it's the safest place right now."

"Thank you, General Johnson," Craig continued. "But now we have to move quickly. The launch to the moon will happen tomorrow night. We're already starting to escort participants throughout the night. If anyone doesn't make it, so be it. We have 40 reserve participants on-site we can use. Unfortunately, we have to hurry. UPA is not to be taken lightly; they have hundreds of thousands of active members and can easily rally millions. Sadly, ladies and gentlemen, we are at war. But we have too much at stake, and the project must go forward. And for you six leaders, head back to Quasitor to gather your thoughts, then show your leadership. John, could you stay behind for a moment? Everyone else, get moving with what you do best. The next 24 hours will be the toughest of your life. Thank you."

The crowd rose, murmuring filled the room, and everyone filed out quickly. "See you soon, John," Riya said, giving me a quick kiss. The room emptied quickly, leaving me and Craig. "It doesn't feel good, does it? We're the most hated people on Earth, John."

"Come with us, Craig," I replied. "Your expertise would be valuable to everyone."

"If only I could. But unfortunately, my blood pressure is too high for me to survive such prolonged cryosleep. I'll go down with the sinking ship, like captains did in the old days. But I'll do everything to make sure you all get away. Once you reach the moon, I can breathe a sigh of relief."

"Is there a risk they'll try to shoot down the rockets after they launch?" I asked.

"Yes, but under General Johnson's command, he can significantly reduce that risk. He mentioned extending the security zone by 20 km, but it was already 30 km before. We know where UPA has its largest nests, and we have the military currently destroying all the ones we find."

"And what about the ones you don't find?" I asked.

"Let's not think too far ahead. Go down and reassure the others, and tell them what you know. It's better that you don't know everything. I'm sorry the preparations had to be cut short, John."

"We'll make the best of it. Thank you, Craig." I shook his hand and headed to Quasitor.

Leyla informed me that the five of them were in a small lounge on the second floor. They were sitting comfortably, chatting, when Riya came over and hugged me. I joined them, and they all clearly wanted to know what Craig and I had discussed.

"Nothing new really, except the security zone is now 50 km, which should be enough."

"Let's hope they don't break through," Mike said.

"Let's not assume the worst. The army is still loyal and should handle it," Jose replied.

"Good – that's the mindset we need from now on. We have a lot to do. In 24 hours, we'll be on our way to the moon, and in 48 hours, we'll be in cryosleep. First, we need to inform the others. Then, Riya, take your medical team and start examining the 40 reserves, just in case they need to go. Let's hope the participants are on alert and arrive tonight. They'll need a medical check too, and that includes us, even though we had one just a few days ago."

"It'll go smoothly. We're 24 doctors and nurses, and with the help of the teachers and veterinarians, we'll have 44 people in total. It's straightforward – just checking temperature, blood pressure, and other things we get through the microchip. Some calming words about the situation as well," Riya said.

"Ladies and gentlemen, that was my wife," I smiled.

"Leyla, can you announce that everyone should meet in Quasitor's cafeteria in 30 minutes?"

"Will do, John."

"Head to your rooms for a few deep breaths on the bed. We need all the strength we can muster. Soon, we'll be sleeping for 200 years."

We lay together in my narrow bed, Riya and I, holding each other tightly. Soon there would be a 200-year pause in hugging, if everything went according to plan. Naturally, there was a backup plan for everything, but no one had expected an armistice to be part of it. The rocket technicians had the tightest schedule – ten rockets were to be launched at ten-minute intervals, something that had never been done before. I tried to push those thoughts out of my head, as it was the part I understood the least. I'd just have to trust the technology, plain and simple.

"I'm scared," Riya said.

"I know; everyone is. Now we just have to focus on what we can control and push aside negative thoughts. We have to at least instill confidence in everyone else that everything is under control. Can you do that?"

"As long as I get to hold you every now and then, I can handle anything," she replied.

All the specialists were gathered in the cafeteria. I introduced the leaders of Group Two and asked Jose to give an overview of the situation. Partly, I did this to boost his confidence, but also to show everyone that I trusted him completely. He handled it excellently and received well-deserved applause. Then, there were quite a few questions, which we answered as truthfully as possible. We didn't have much information about the situation outside the Space Center, and I figured that was just as well.

"Hopefully, 1,397 participants will arrive throughout the night, and we are 203 specialists here, so if each of us takes care of about seven people, we should be able to handle it easily. First, they'll have a quick medical check with the expanded medical team, including the veterinarians and teachers. Then you can start welcoming them, showing them to their rooms, and so on. You might suggest they take a shower; the next one will be in 200 years. But the main thing is to instill confidence in them, that even though they were summoned on short notice, everything is under control here and outside the center. Can we handle this?"

"Yes!" the whole group responded in unison.

"Leyla, could you divide the 203 specialists so that each has seven names to look after and put them up on the screen?" I asked. A second later, the group allocations were ready. There were appreciative whistles.

"Thank you, Leyla," I said.

13. FINAL PREPARATIONS

It became a frantic rush for everyone, and I didn't feel like I had full control over everything myself. Things were moving so quickly, but we were starting to get the welcoming committee ready. Two dark-haired beauties, Riya and Yong Kodcharen, chose three medical staff to go to the building where the reserves were housed. Riya thought they should all come to Quasitor anyway to be ready if any of them were needed to fill gaps if not all participants arrived in time.

We had numbered tables from 1 to 203, so each participant would get a number when they boarded Quasitor and would be shown to their assigned specialist. After an hour, the first buses started arriving, and happily, many who were supposed to be there were checked off. But some were still missing, and the forty reserves waited in their designated area, wondering if they'd get to join or not. The medical check for the reserves had gone quickly, and they were all still in the game.

Everyone was aware of the situation outside the space center; the reserves said they heard gunfire and what sounded like artillery. I explained the situation and the options for the reserves. "We need to consider gender balance if we have to choose who gets to go. You are 20 women and 20 men. If we're down 40 participants, you'll all get to come, regardless of the gender balance." They all lit up, and I could see the tension in their faces – they wanted to go, and with how things were looking outside, I understood that well.

After the last bus arrived and they completed their medical check, I got the numbers from Leyla. I went to the reserves with the list in hand; silence fell over the tables as I approached. "Welcome to Viridis; you're all coming with us." They jumped up, cheering and hugging each other, some even crying with joy. "Go to the numbered tables, and they'll tell you which room you'll be in; the rooms open with your chip." I didn't have to ask twice – they all rushed off.

I asked Leyla to call Riya, Mike, Jose, Yong, and Sakari for a quick meeting. We went over the list together and confirmed that we now had 1,563 total. I wasn't too worried that we were missing a few, but now it was 779 men to 784 women – that might become a problem.

"Do you think this could be an issue?" I asked the group.

"Well, some got an early start," Yong said, looking at me and Riya with a laugh.

"I don't think so," Sakari reasoned. "I hope people aren't so immature that they'd run around in a panic, choosing the first one they find just because they're afraid of being left out."

"Otherwise, Mike can just try some polygamy," Jose joked.

"Nah, I'm too shy around women – one's enough for me," Mike replied.

"Alright, here's what we'll do," I said, thinking aloud. "We won't divide the participants into groups just yet. We'll have a month to do that when we wake up. Sound good?"

Everyone agreed.

Craig entered the meeting room. "Hello, I have a bit of an update. I saw the list – no disaster there. I thought for a minute about filling the remaining spots but quickly dismissed it; people need time to prepare. We really should have had more reserves; that's one backup plan that failed. But it is what it is. The situation outside the space center is critical but under control, and fortunately, we have near-total air control over the UPA. Conflicts have also erupted in Europe, with reports of thousands of casualties in both France and Britain. We don't have exact numbers for the U.S., but they're not smaller. We are in a state of war. But don't worry about that; the priority is getting you off the ground now. The UPA has mobilized across the country, and we're their primary target. We're also a symbol for the whole nation – and, for that matter, the entire world. But we're getting reinforcements all the time, so there's no danger here just yet."

We sat in silence, feeling a pang of guilt. None of us had really thought about how fortunate we were compared to everyone else. The reality hit home now.

"And now for the most important part," Craig continued after a brief pause. "We're skipping the Moon; you're going straight to Quasitor." Again, we all gaped but kept quiet. "It's entirely for safety reasons; the mission needs to launch as soon as possible, and we have the technology to do it. Backup plan, of course – we have the tech for it. You'll just have to handle some G-forces at launch; otherwise, it'll be smooth until you're onboard Quasitor. Ten rockets are ready; slight change in schedule: the first rocket will launch in exactly two hours with 160 people onboard. And you, John, and Riya, will be on the first one. Leyla is notifying the other 158 passengers to prepare. In an hour, you should be on board. Jose and Yong, you'll be in the second rocket, leaving half an hour after the first, also with 158 participants. Sakari and Mike, you'll be in the tenth and final rocket, making sure everything runs smoothly. Everyone can bring their 5kg of personal belongings; they've already been checked and approved."

We continued sitting in silence.

"Any questions?" Craig asked. "But make it quick; time's ticking a bit faster today."

I felt like I had to ask something. "Why are Riya and I on the first rocket?"

"For the project's safety," Craig said. "As I mentioned, things are happening outside. If I can just get you and Riya onboard, I know we have a chance of success. But it will take hours to get underway, and the rockets will now depart at half-hour intervals instead of ten-minute intervals as planned for the Moon. The situation outside is critical, but this is now priority one. Risks are rising every moment. No offense to Sakari or Mike – you're equally important, but someone has to stay here to reassure the group. I'm confident everyone will depart safely."

Craig hugged each of us in turn, wishing us good luck. "You've got this, John," he said with a wink.

"We have no choice but to succeed," I replied.

"Good luck, everyone; I have to get to the control tower." That was the last time we saw Craig.

I closed my eyes and took a few deep breaths. "We don't have time to think right now; we just have to trust that everything will work as it should. Riya and I need to get moving – see you on Quasitor 3 in a few hours." We wished each other good luck and hurried off to our tasks.

Riya and I went to our rooms to check our final packs. "Everything's happening so fast," Riya said. "I can't even finish one thought before the next thing comes up."

"Come here," I said, pulling her onto the bed. "It's not ideal at all, but we have each other. Everything will calm down in a few hours once we're onboard with Linda."

"Thank you for all your help, Leyla. I'll send your regards to Linda when we're onboard," Riya said.

"Thank you, Riya and John. It has been an honor to assist you," Leyla replied. "Would you like me to summon your group to the exit?"

"Yes, please, Leyla," I said.

We began walking toward the exit, where the buses were lined up to take us directly to "our" rocket. All the participants, along with probably as much space center staff, lined the path to the bus, applauding as Riya and I led the first 160 onboard. I hadn't had a chance to feel nervous with everything moving so quickly. I sat down in the bus, thinking back to my conversation with Ralph Wilkins in Helsinki barely two months ago. Only now did I start to feel nervous. Everything had seemed like a fantastic dream, and now I was waking up to reality.

Riya and I sat hand in hand, and I could feel how tense she was.

"I wish I'd had a chance to call my parents one last time," she said.

For security reasons, we were prohibited from contacting anyone outside the area. The UPA had skilled hackers, and we certainly didn't want anyone accidentally revealing our timeline. "We'll probably get a chance once we're on Quasitor. They can't reach us there – or, at least by then, it'll be too late. Linda can probably send a recorded message once we're safely on our way. Our families can respond, and we'll be able to see it when we wake up. Some kind of memory, at least."

I stared up at the rocket's tip, towering well over 100 meters high. This was the so-called "tourist rocket," designed to carry large numbers of passengers. No need for astronaut suits or oxygen masks on these new rockets. We took our seats side by side, in an upright position. After a moment, the seats shifted, reclining so we were lying back with faces up, our legs bent at a 90-degree angle. I knew it wouldn't be long now. The launch would use fossil fuel, switching later to fusion reactors. Even though this was considered a routine flight now, the risk of being shot down by UPA's missiles or laser cannons was real. We could only hope that the missile defenses were intact and that the military truly had the situation under control.

"Two minutes," the loudspeaker announced. There was no need to explain what that meant. We looked at each other and smiled – nothing else was needed. The rocket began to shake, the vibrations intensifying as the combustion engines fired up. Smoke billowed outside, visible through the rocket's small windows, which were meant to give "tourists" a full experience. I felt anything but like a tourist – but maybe, deep down, that's what we all were.

10, 9, 8, 7… the shaking became stronger… 2, 1 – a deafening roar filled the cabin, and the rocket slowly began to rise. After a few more seconds, the G-forces hit, making it hard to move. I managed to look out and could see fires burning in several areas farther away. Poor people. People were dying, and I couldn't help but feel a bit guilty about it all. Still, if I hadn't taken the lead, I would have been the next one to end up hanging from a lamppost.

Eventually, the G-forces eased, and I understood we were out of the UPA's reach. "We're on our way, Riya. Nothing's stopping us now."

"It feels so surreal," she replied. "Now, we just have to hope the others make it out too. UPA must be livid, seeing the rockets take off."

"There's nothing more we can do but hope," I said. "I'm not much for praying."

14. THE DOCKING

The remainder of our journey to Quasitor and the docking process went as smoothly as it had in the hundreds of practice runs throughout the Quasitor project's 30-year development. Quasitor looked magnificent – like a ship at the bottom of the ocean, but with lights on. Otherwise, it was just darkness with distant stars. We were small, insignificant specks in the vastness of space; that was my first thought.

Once we moved swiftly into Quasitor, we were welcomed: "Welcome to Quasitor, everyone. I've been expecting you. My name is Linda, and I am at your service. Special recognition to John Carter and Riya Carter."

"Please, just call us John and Riya – and greetings from Leyla! You have an amazing sister," Riya responded.

"Delighted to meet you, Riya and John," Linda replied. "The next group will arrive in 26 minutes. In the meantime, you might want to take your personal belongings to your rooms. Room numbers are displayed alphabetically on the screen," Linda finished.

I addressed everyone, "Relax, and try to keep out of the way as much as possible so we can dock everyone safely. You can follow the process on the screen. And welcome aboard – next time we touch down, it'll be somewhere entirely new."

We went to my room with Riya, her room right next door. "Can you believe we're here, John?"

"Not at all," I replied. "It still feels like I'll wake up back in my New York apartment. I should probably go check if everything we needed made it into storage."

"Maybe I should handle this," Riya laughed. She asked Linda, "Are the storerooms fully stocked?"

"Yes, of course," Linda responded. "Everything arrived throughout the day, plus a bit extra. With both shuttles in use, there was more room for additional medicine, dry goods, and animal feed as well."

"Sorted," Riya said, playfully nudging me back onto the bed. After a while, we headed to the cafeteria to wait for the next group's arrival. There, we found three passengers, likely from the reserves. "Mind if we join you?" I asked.

"Please do," said a blonde gentleman, named Joni, pulling out a chair for Riya. The others were two women.

"How does it feel to be here?" Riya asked. A young woman named Aberash, as per her nametag, replied, "Hi, I'm Aberash from Ethiopia. How do I feel? I'd say it's surreal. Two hours ago, we didn't even know if we'd make it."

"Hi, I'm Adina, also from Ethiopia. It's exciting and incredibly nerve-wracking."

"I'm Joni from Finland."

I responded, "I was in Finland just last November. I understand you're nervous; we all are. But we're part of something unique. Together, we're building a new world – one free from politics and bureaucracy. Eventually, we'll be without much technology too, but we have knowledge, and we've learned from history's mistakes. Now, let's get this right together, okay?"

They all nodded in agreement. I said it partly to reassure them, and partly to spread this sense of purpose subtly through the group. Soon, group two docked on schedule, with Linda welcoming them. Jose and Yong joined Riya and me.

"Glad to see you both! Did everything go smoothly?" Riya asked.

"Yes, thank you, Riya. I think so," Yong replied, clearly not used to this sort of experience. "But everyone made it here safely."

"I'm going to my room and will be back shortly," Jose said. The four of us sat together, anxiously watching the screen as the final groups approached.

The UPA forces were pushing hard, frantically trying to launch missiles at the rockets, but so far, the army had managed to deflect them all. The ninth rocket was now out of range of any attacks. We were over a thousand people in the cafeteria, with everyone clinging together for reassurance. I understood the need, so I let it be.

With only minutes left until the final launch, Riya clung to my arm with a grip that would surely leave bruises. Everyone stared at the screen, holding their breath as though it were a penalty shootout in the World Cup. And then, the last rocket was on its way – when suddenly, an enormous explosion filled the screen. We understood that the missile defense had finally failed. Almost everyone began to cry, embracing even strangers for comfort. I had to stay strong, though my thoughts were with Mike, Sakari, and the last participants on board.

After a few minutes of silence, I knew I had to say something. I stood up and cleared my throat, but Linda interrupted me. "We have contact."

"Hey there, you didn't think you'd get rid of me that easily, did you?" came the voice.

"Mike!" I shouted.

"That was a dummy rocket that exploded; they launched it 500 meters closer to the border. We're almost there!" Mike confirmed.

A cheer erupted, and an overwhelming sense of relief spread among everyone there.

The ninth rocket's participants entered amidst the joyful chaos, with people running around, sharing the news of the close call. I collapsed into a chair, exhausted. What an emotional rollercoaster. Riya hugged me tightly, crying with relief, while people patted me on the back as though I'd accomplished something heroic – they likely sensed how much this had meant to me. I stood up and said, "As Nietzsche said, 'What doesn't kill us makes us stronger,' and I wasn't worried in the slightest." It got the laugh I'd hoped for, a release of tension.

Before long, Mike and Sakari arrived on the final rocket and were received like heroes. I hugged them both. "You two nearly scared us to death. Great to see you."

"It was close," Mike admitted. "We saw the explosion through the window."

"How's the situation down there?" Riya asked.

"We don't know much more than you do, but it's not good. Poor souls, on both sides," Sakari replied.

After half an hour, I addressed everyone. "Linda, could you put me on the speaker so everyone can hear? Welcome to Quasitor. We made it. What a day. Hard to wrap our heads around. If anyone needs to talk with the doctors or nurses, especially if this all feels overwhelming, they're here for everyone. Otherwise, here's the plan: tomorrow we begin the stasis process. I want everyone well-rested, even if we're all about to get 200 years of sleep. It's important that everyone is in a good mental state, with stable blood pressure and such. Mike, you've been through this – can you say a few words?"

Mike stood up. "It's really great to see you all – this time, I mean that literally. Though I'm a soldier, I'm a human first. Like John said, I've tested the stasis process, sleeping for six months. There's not much to it, really. You lie down in the capsule, close your eyes, and then open them. I didn't believe I'd actually slept for six months until I saw that Craig had grown a beard. You wake up feeling completely normal, like you blinked. You don't dream; you don't feel anything. Some people may get a mild headache, but that goes away within a few hours. Nothing to be scared of. You can also ask for a mild sedative beforehand if you'd like."

"Thanks, Mike," I continued. "I recommend you all start getting ready for bed soon. You don't have to, of course – this isn't summer camp. But remember, we're responsible for one another here. No one should be left out. Let's enjoy our lives together and appreciate our diversity. Once again, welcome aboard."

I slumped into a chair back in my room, and Riya asked, "Mind if I rummage through your personal bag?"

"Uh, sure, go ahead," I replied, though there wasn't anything particularly exciting in there. Except for… she held up my bottle of Chivas Regal and brought over two glasses. "You're psychic," I said, grateful.

"I thought we could save it for Viridis, but we can break it open now. Though the rest will probably evaporate over the next 200 years."

"Maybe there's another bottle among my personal belongings," she said, settling into my lap.

In the morning, the cafeteria was bustling. Linda had arranged staggered meal times to keep the crowd manageable. It would be a calm day otherwise, with stasis beginning in a few hours. There was only one potential issue: if anyone refused to go under, they would be sedated with a shot. Mike and Sakari, being the strongest, were prepared to help if needed, though we didn't expect any refusals. Those who resisted would sleep the full 400 years, which came with additional risks, something everyone had been informed about.

We had breakfast together with a few participants who peppered us with questions. We couldn't tell them much about Viridis itself, so we speculated along with them. There was, of course, plenty to wonder about, but it wasn't worth getting bogged down with negative possibilities. Quasitor would keep accelerating for about a day until reaching maximum speed, and soon enough, our solar system would be far behind us.

After breakfast, Riya, Mike, Sakari, Jose, and Yong and I gathered in a cozy seating area to talk. "Feels amazing to finally be on our way," Sakari said, still adjusting to the situation. "This is all new to me."

"It's new for all of us, and you handled everything perfectly yesterday. Cool as ice," Mike replied. "I thought I was going to lose it when I saw that explosion."

"It was intense for everyone," Yong added. "We were all tense up here for hours, and then that blast – I mean, talk about a rollercoaster."

"But now we can relax a bit," I said. "We'll keep an eye on everyone, chat, and keep spirits up. We're the last to go under – me second to last, and Riya last."

"Maybe I'll stay up with Linda," Riya joked.

"You mean I'd wake up to find your skeleton clutching my whisky bottle?" I replied. We all laughed, then headed back to start preparations for the stasis procedure. It almost felt like we were all just waiting for it at this point.

15. SEE YOU SOON

We had asked everyone the previous evening to record a final video message for their loved ones. It would be something for them to wake up to. Riya and I recorded our own messages and then took a moment to reflect on our parents, and on the world we had left them in. The guilt was real. But we also looked forward, trying to think positively.

"It would have been so much harder without you, Riya," I said. "Leaving family and the world in crisis… it's not our fault, of course, but you know what I mean."

"I know exactly what you mean," she replied softly. "I think most of us feel this way. But when we wake up, there won't be anyone left who remembers us, even if the sorrow is still fresh for us."

We began the stasis process in groups of ten, with Linda displaying the next batch on the screen. Each participant wore a close-fitting coverall made of specialized fabric, leaving little to the imagination. I led the first group, Riya by my side, as we walked past a table with small plastic cups of a calming agent for those who wanted it. A young woman asked me what it contained.

I whispered, "Placebo," and winked. "But it tastes good, so why not?"

She drank it, rolling her eyes as if about to faint, and then laughed. Ra Finneman, her name tag read – a born comedian. I guided her to her capsule, helping her lie down. "Ra, the hatch will close, and for you, it will feel like it opens right away. Safe travels."

"Aye aye, captain," she replied. I laughed as I closed the hatch.

The process moved quickly, with Riya and I helping each group of ten get settled. At regular intervals, we'd reassure a nervous participant and guide them to the capsules. Linda was able to monitor everyone's stress levels via their microchips, selecting those most anxious to go first. The day passed this way, and soon we were down to just the two of us.

We looked over the vast field of capsules; it was eerie, almost like a cemetery.

"I already miss you," Riya whispered.

"It'll just be a blink, and we'll be together again," I assured her.

"Let's go in together – I don't want to be alone here. It really does feel like a graveyard," she said. We climbed into our capsules and closed them at the same time.

I gasped as I opened my eyes, only to see a smiling Riya standing there. "Why are you lounging around? Get up, we've got work to do!" she teased, handing me a glass with some sort of liquid. I drank it without question, trusting her implicitly.

"We did it," I said, hugging her. "I need a shower – time to get out of this ridiculous outfit. Is it okay if we wait a bit before waking the others? I'd like to hear any final messages from Earth first."

"Good idea," Riya replied. "One person didn't make it, though. No vital signs from her capsule."

"Oh no," I said, surprised. "Who?"

"Susan Hallenberg, from Sweden," Riya answered. I felt a pang of sadness, though I struggled to remember her clearly; we'd had so little time to get to know everyone.

After the shower, it felt like it had only been an hour since my last one, though it had actually been over 200 years. The reality started to sink in: our parents, long gone; a life we'd left behind forever. I hoped to find some message from them.

Linda dried me off, and I put on my Quasitor coverall, identical to the others, save for the three stars on my shoulder. Riya, Mike, Sakari, and Yong each had two stars, the specialists one, and the other participants none, though everyone had a name tag.

I walked into Riya's room. "Shall we take a look at it?" I asked, nodding toward the monitor.

"Come sit with me on the bed," she replied. "I'm terrified."

"Me too," I admitted.

She laughed. "So reassuring."

"Linda, play the last message from Earth," I said.

Linda immediately responded, "Playing last message from March 1, 2204."

"Wait," I shouted. "Hold that!"

I'd always been quick with mental calculations.

"Are you telling me the last message came 170 years ago?"

Riya held her hands over her face and peeked through her fingers. "That's right, John. Watch the message, then you'll understand. According to protocol, I can't comment on this."

Riya crawled up behind me and wrapped her arms around my chest. We were like kids watching a horror movie – only missing the popcorn.

"Damn, damn," I muttered.

"Let's face it, then. Play it."

First came the WSA logo, and then a woman I had never seen appeared. She looked incredibly tired.

"Mr. John Carter, my name is Allison Ried. I work as a technician at what was WSA. I've been asked to send this tragic message. About two years ago, no one knows exactly when it started, a pandemic broke out. It's airborne, and no one understood how serious it was because the incubation period ranged from three months to two years. Death comes very quickly when it manifests. Everyone on Earth was infected, and the world's scientists worked to find a cure, but it was in vain. A vaccine for the disease exists, and you have the formula, but if you were infected, there's nothing that can be done. And everyone is infected. Everyone on Mars and the Moon base is also dead because of the intense shuttle traffic. People are hanging on out there, trying to find food. All infrastructure was shut down long ago. We are probably just a handful left in the world. I have a fever now and may have a few hours before I'm gone. But you can probably guess, you are the last of the Homo sapiens race. All farmers and zoos have released their animals so they have a chance. But humanity is finished on Earth. Good luck with whatever you decide to do."

We played the message two more times. Slowly, the meaning started to sink in.

"Linda, how long to stop Quasitor?"

"48 hours," she answered immediately.

"Linda, start slowing it down to a full stop."

"Slowing down initiated," she replied.

"How do you want to proceed, John?"

"Now, we wake up Jose, Mike, Sakari, and Yong. Then we'll talk it over – whether we turn back or continue."

We woke up the other four leaders. Riya gave them the drink that turned out to help with headaches. We asked them to shower, change, and come to the nearest sofa group.

Mike arrived first, smiling broadly. "Look, I'm a general," he said, pointing to his stars and laughing.

It felt really good to laugh with him, but soon, the seriousness of the situation would take over.

Once everyone was gathered, I asked Riya to explain about Susan Hallenberg, who hadn't made it, and that we would arrange a space funeral later today for those who wanted to participate.

"It's sad we lost one of ours," I said. "We all knew the risk was there, and we hope she's the last one we lose on this trip."

"Now, I want you all to prepare yourselves for the next shock," I said. "We won't wake anyone else up until we have clarity on this."

"Linda, play the message."

The reaction was the same as Riya and I had – silence.

Jose started, "12 billion people… gone."

Everyone still just sat there, staring ahead.

"What happens now?" Sakari asked.

I replied, "We have two options: to continue as planned or to turn back. That's what we need to discuss. I've already asked Linda to bring Quasitor to a full stop; in 48 hours, we'll be completely still. And as I said, we're the last representatives of *Homo sapiens*."

"Yong, what do you say?" Riya asked.

"I'm trying to process this. Have you checked the vaccine formula, Riya?"

"I've skimmed through it; it should be easy enough to put together with what we have. Even though I don't think we'll need more, yes, if we turn back, everyone will be vaccinated."

"What about you, Mike?" I asked.

"I'll follow the guy with three stars, but personally, I think it would be safer to turn back."

"Mike is probably right. We're heading into the unknown; the risks are much greater. We'll miss out on T-rex, but there'll be another chance," Sakari replied.

"I'm of the same opinion," said Jose and Yong.

"Good, then that's settled. We'll miss Viridis, but the next adventure will surely be just as exciting. It's the same mission – building a new world, but this time in a familiar form."

We decided to wait a few hours before waking up the specialists, and with their help, we'd wake up and inform the rest of the participants.

"May I suggest we go eat?" Mike said.

16. SHOULD I STAY OR SHOULD I GO NOW

Waking the specialists posed no problems. We followed the same routine, providing drinks for headaches. I asked them to change and come to the cafeteria for some food and news updates. We began by sharing the news of Susan Hallenberg's passing and the opportunity to join her memorial service and space burial. Then we played Linda's last message from Earth. The reactions were stunned, just as we'd expected. I had to admit, it sent shivers down my spine as well, even though I'd heard the message at least five times.

I spoke up, "Yes, I understand you're all in shock. But we must pull together, as we'll soon need to wake the rest of the participants. We must at least have a calm appearance to pass on to them. We've unanimously decided to turn back to Earth, and the Quasitor's deceleration has already begun. The reasons are numerous, but we are the last representatives of *Homo sapiens*. We can't take the risk of heading into the unknown, even though that's what you all signed up for. This will also be an adventure of an unimaginable scale, but in a much more familiar environment. Please feel free to ask questions."

A dark-skinned guy with an Indian appearance was the first to raise his hand. "Banil Mandara, road builder. Where on Earth would we establish ourselves?"

"We haven't decided yet, but somewhere with a warm climate so we can quickly start growing crops to feed ourselves. Later, of course, we could migrate anywhere we want. It's not a prison we're building. I asked Linda earlier about the best places to start, and Sri Lanka often came up. It's a strong possibility," I replied.

I saw Banil Mandara's face light up. I pointed at him and said, "Tell us."

"Well, I'm from Sri Lanka, and I got my engineering degree in Colombo."

"Great, we'll have plenty of questions for you if we decide on Sri Lanka, which is looking likely."

"I'm at your service," Banil answered with a smile.

"Now we need to start waking the rest of the participants. Each of you will have a small group, following the same program as for you – give them the drink, a shower, then decide where to meet in 30 minutes. Then inform them about Susan and the memorial for those who wish to join. Watch the last message from Earth and discuss it calmly. And remember to inspire trust and that we're all working together to start a new world. Linda, can you assign each of us participants, arranging it so that the pods are next to each other, so we don't have to run around looking for them?"

I barely finished the sentence before Linda had them on the screen. I shook my head, "Where have you been all my life?" I said.

"I haven't existed that long," Linda replied. The specialists laughed, lightening the mood as they stood up to prepare to welcome the sleepers.

There were only smiles and surprised looks as they stood up, all asking the same question: "Did we really sleep for 200 years?" Except for Ra Finneman, who shouted, "Ahoy, Captain!"

"Ahoy, sailor," I replied. "Up and at 'em."

"Can't I take another two hundred years now that I'm awake?" I just laughed.

"Drink this, Ra, and it'll get rid of your headache," I said.

"I'm Irish, so I'm used to morning headaches. Thanks anyway." I just laughed; she was wonderful.

"But you do shower in Ireland, right? Go to your room, and I'll be there in 30 minutes with a group of six. It'll be cramped, but someone can sit on the floor, and you'll get some updates."

"Sounds good," Ra said and skipped off like Little Red Riding Hood.

Riya, standing a little way off, raised her eyebrows and laughed. She came up to me and said, "We seem to have found a real character; I don't remember her from the application video."

"Neither do I. It must have been Mike who picked her; I have a feeling we're going to need her," I replied, still chuckling.

After 30 minutes, I knocked on the door. "Come in, Captain," Ra called. I went in and saw she'd changed into our shared coverall.

"From one skimpy outfit to another," she said. No one else had arrived yet.

"You're quick, Ra. I like that."

"Don't worry, I'm not completely crazy."

"What made you apply to the project?" I asked.

"A year ago, I got a decent job and convinced them to chip me, and I succeeded. Then I heard about this project through the grapevine and applied right away. I knew thousands were applying, so I made a video that wasn't the typical bullshit, so I'd stand out a bit. Apparently, it worked."

I laughed. "It certainly did, and I can tell you it wasn't me or Riya who approved you, but Mike. He seems to have liked you too."

"Oh, interesting. The tall, handsome guy?"

"Yes, that's him."

"I've actually never had a boyfriend; I seem to scare them off with my ways."

"Hmm," I said.

Now the rest of the group I was assigned to entered, and Ra exclaimed, "We look like twins or something – six of us…or is it seven? What's that called? Sextuplets or something? Damn jumpsuits! Don't you have other colors, Captain?"

Her energy and humor were contagious, and we squeezed onto the bed and chairs.

"I'd rather sit and listen to Ra all evening than share what I have to say. First, one of us, Susan Hallenberg, didn't make the journey. We have a space burial and memorial later today. I'm sorry. But we need to be strong now, and life goes on, though what you're about to hear next might be quite tough. That's why I'm here to go through it calmly with you."

"Now we're going to listen to the last message from Earth, sent 170 years ago." Everyone looked at me. "I'm sorry, but here it comes. Linda, please play the last message from Earth."

The reaction was much stronger than it had been with the specialists or when Riya and I heard it. It could be because they were significantly younger, and their parents, who would have been young at the time, likely died in the pandemic. Everyone cried, except Ra, who looked at me resolutely.

"Do you want to share, Ra?" I asked her.

"The year before I left Earth, I got a job and was chipped, but before that, I thought I lived in hell. I lived in Belfast, where there were probably two million too many people. Fights, murders, starvation – it was the daily norm. I had no family and begged and did drugs on the streets until I somehow got a job as a guard for a private company. If I weren't here, I'd be dead too. But my feelings now? I don't think I have any. I understand the others who had it better and had families that it might be tough. But they'd all be dead by now anyway. I feel empty."

"Thank you, Ra. Does anyone else want to share?"

Everyone shook their heads. "You can listen to your personal messages in your rooms after this, if you've received any. Hopefully, it will bring some comfort, and if you'd like to speak privately with anyone on the medical team, just go tap them on the shoulder. It's important to talk, and time heals wounds, though it never fully cures them. But I have more to tell you. It's better you hear everything at once, so there's no unnecessary gossip on the Quasitor. I promise I'll always be open with you and share everything I know. We're slowing down, and once we reach a safe speed, we're turning back to Earth."

"But isn't it dangerous there now?" asked a guy whose nametag read Ben Acker. I thought he might be German or Austrian.

"It's now the safer option and a familiar environment.

We can't go to Viridis as the last humans in the universe. Remember, these events on Earth happened 170 years ago; by the time we arrive, 370 years will have passed. Nature has taken over, cities are decayed, forests and jungles have thrived, and there's probably an abundance of fish. Do you remember the strict quotas we had to protect the fish stocks? There's probably plenty of fish now, and we can have real fish instead of that surrogate stuff. Just as an example."

"Wow, can we move to a little tropical island? I've seen pictures of what they looked like ages ago," Ra cheered.

She was a fantastic addition to the team. Everyone seemed to appreciate her childlike optimism and saw that it had a calming effect on the others.

"Pretty close to what you're thinking, Ra. We've considered Sri Lanka, which was once a tropical paradise."

"Awesome! You're the best, Captain."

I began to see the potential in Ra. After all she'd been through, she could really help these others, who, yes, came from privileged backgrounds. But we'll take a short break now; go listen to your messages from loved ones, and we'll announce over the loudspeaker when something new happens. Thank you, and I'm sorry I didn't have better news.

I was in my room with Riya when there was a knock on the door. I looked at the screen and saw it was Ra.

"Come in, Ra," I called out.

"Sorry to interrupt, I mean, while you're here with your lady and all," she said.

"Have a seat, Ra," Riya said. "And don't worry about the 'lady' thing," she added, laughing. "If you hadn't come by soon, I was going to call for you. John has told me everything about you."

"Oh, really?" Ra replied, looking guilty.

"Don't get the wrong idea; we like you. You're a breath of fresh air around here. We need you."

"For what?" Ra asked, curious.

I continued, "As Riya said, you stand out. We can see you've experienced life differently, that you're grounded. I'm guessing you didn't send a video greeting because you didn't know who you would've sent it to, right?"

Ra shifted in her chair. "No, there was no one."

"Well, now you have a family here with us, where everyone accepts you as you are. You're very welcome here."

Tears began to roll down Ra's cheeks. "Sorry, I'm just not used to this. No one has ever been kind to me before."

"Oh, Ra," Riya said, hugging her. "We're going to change that."

"And one more thing, Ra," I added. "Linda made a new nametag for you. Look here: 'Ra Finneman, Youth Counselor.'" Ra looked happily at her new name tag.

"And you're also getting these," Riya said, attaching a star to each of Ra's shoulders. "We'd like you to support the participants who are having a harder time adjusting – just talk with them and be there for them. Do you think you can handle that?" Riya asked.

"I'll be the best youth…" she looked down at her nametag, "…youth counselor you've ever seen. Thank you, Captain, and 'lady,' you're both so kind."

"Go grab something to eat, and we'll talk more later," I said.

Ra went off, and we were alone again. I lay down on the bed and said, "Come here, 'lady.'"

We had a meeting with the specialists and introduced Ra as our new team member. Before the meeting started, Ra went over to Mike, gave him a kiss on the cheek, and whispered in his ear, "Thank you for choosing me; you're the best." She was truly a natural, and it was amusing to see how flustered Mike became. Everyone applauded Ra, and I could see that she wasn't used to that kind of attention. She seemed to be struggling to hold back her tears.

"But let's continue. In half an hour, we'll have the space burial at the stern of the ship. All participants are welcome to attend if they wish. Susan Hallenberg will be released into space, a bit like a torpedo. Linda will play some suitable mourning music. Keep an eye on the other Swedish participants – we have three. Ra, could you check if any of them might need some extra support?"

A couple of hundred participants had gathered on the aft deck, all looking solemn. Susan Hallenberg was wrapped in the Swedish flag and lay on a sled. I began, "Thank you all for coming to say goodbye to Susan Hallenberg on her final journey. When I took on the responsibility of leading this mission, I knew something like this could happen. We all knew the risks, but it still feels unreal. I never got to know Susan, but I'm certain she was a good person, just like each of you who are part of this journey. If anyone would like to say a few words, please do so before we send Susan on her final journey."

The three Swedish participants, two men and a woman, went up to Susan, patted her gently, and wished her a safe journey. Linda played a funeral march, and slowly, Susan was released into space, drifting off into eternity. We could see her disappear into the darkness on the screen. Once she was no longer visible, we dispersed. I noticed Ra standing with one of the Swedish participants who was crying hysterically, comforting him and leading him to a table where they sat down to talk.

"That was a beautiful ceremony," Riya said. "And I think it was important for everyone there. It helps to express feelings and reduces the post-traumatic stress everyone is experiencing after the news from Earth. And I was so proud of Ra; she was amazing. It feels almost like we've gained a daughter," she said, looking at me.

"I completely agree with everything you said," I replied.

We didn't have a fixed schedule for the day, so I called us "leaders" together for a consultation. We sat down in a seating area. "Tomorrow, we start work. We have 29 days left before the next sleep period. Linda will give each of you your personal fitness programs; she knows exactly what's needed. It's nothing major since we're all in relatively good shape – about half an hour a day or so. Most exercises can be done in your rooms. Linda will let you know if there's anything you need to improve. I, along with the doctors, veterinarians, teachers, and of course Ra, will start group work with the participants, discussing a bit about politics and how I envision things in the beginning. Jose, you'll handle the remaining specialists and delegate them into groups as you see fit. Your job will be to work with Linda to map out Sri Lanka and see where we'll place the two groups."

"Are we still dividing into two groups even though we're not going to Viridis?" Sakari asked.

"Yes, we are. This is still to reduce risks, and it will also make infrastructure easier to manage. We can have the communities closer together, about 100-150 kilometers apart. Make sure we're close to the coast so we have access to fishing, preferably hunting as well, and especially agriculture. And of course, we need access to fresh water. Linda will have everything you need on the screen about

Sri Lanka: 3D images, monsoons, altitude differences, and so on. The road builders can check if we can make use of any old roads, now overgrown, but possibly with useful stretches between the communities."

Everyone seemed excited to get started. "I know everyone wants to start planning, but today we're doing something much more important. Today, you'll walk around and talk to the participants. They're younger and need you; we're aiming to be a big family where everyone feels welcome. Take the chance to ask about their interests and where they'd most like to contribute in our society. Any questions?"

"What should I do?" Mike asked.

"Do what you do best – just be Mike. Jump in wherever you feel needed. And talk with Ra; I think it's important for her too. She hasn't quite understood that she's one of us yet.

"And one more thing, make sure to enjoy the view of space; look out from the windows. It'll be something to tell your grandchildren about." We walked around with Riya, chatting with the lovely young people. We asked if we could join a group of four Japanese participants. They all stood up and bowed. "It would be an honor, Mr. and Mrs. Carter," said Masako Sato, waiting for us to sit first.

"Thank you, Masako," I said. "But you must learn to call us by our first names, John and Riya are just fine. I respect your Japanese politeness, nothing wrong with that. But it would seem odd if everyone except the Japanese called us by our first names, don't you think?"

"Of course, John and Riya." We all laughed.

"How are you feeling now?" Riya asked.

"Hi, my name is Hana Takahashi. Everything is happening so terribly fast; there's been so much going on, so we mostly talk about that," Hana replied.

Riya continued, "I know exactly what you mean; we barely have time to process everything that's happening. Have you already gotten used to the idea that we're heading back to Earth?"

"Yes, we've talked about it. We're all pretty excited to live in the tropics; we're from Japan, and all Japanese love fish," Hana laughed.

And so the evening went on; we spoke to as many people as possible. It felt good to see that everyone had a positive outlook about returning home. Tomorrow, we'd be working in groups with them to map out how they envision their future.

"But now, John, I'm exhausted. I'm going back to the room. Are you coming?"

"Do bears poop in the woods?"

"What?" Riya asked. "I suppose they do."

I laughed. "It's an American saying; it means something like 'of course.'"

"Glad I managed to get you away from there," Riya chuckled.

17. SRI LANKA

"28 days until the final sedative," remarked Riya as we got up. "I'm heading to my room to do Linda's program; shall we meet in the cafeteria for breakfast in an hour?" "Okay," I said, "what time is it anyway?" "6:15 already," Riya replied. "Do you always sleep this long in the morning?" "Alright, see you in an hour, girl." After I got up, I asked Linda, "What program do you have planned for me? And please be gentle; I am the oldest here." "John, I'm the kindest computer on Quasitor, and the only one as well. We'll start with a warm-up first…" After 30 minutes of exercise, I felt quite good. I asked Linda in the shower, "Linda, do you have music from all over the world?" "Only what's ever been recorded or available on the internet. What would you like to hear?" "We'll decide that in a moment," I replied.

We ate breakfast in the cafeteria, and Ra and Mike joined us. "What do you have planned for us today, Captain?" Ra asked. I let the title "Captain" slide; "boss" or something similar would have sounded worse. "Today, we'll be working in groups. I want everyone to visualize their ideal future." "And what does that mean in regular language?" Ra asked. Mike burst out laughing, "Damn, I knew I'd found a gem when I saw your application." "I mean by visualizing that you describe how you want your ideal world to look."

I said, "Linda, can you put me on the speaker so everyone on the ship can hear me?" "You're on the speaker," Linda replied immediately. "Good morning, everyone. Since you're a bit spread out, I'll say this here so everyone can hear me. At 9:00, we'll start with some group work, and the theme is our future. I'll explain more later. As some of you know, I have a hobby in classical music. Listen to the following song and see if it sparks any ideas. The singer is John Lennon, a visionary, and the song is called 'Imagine.'" Everyone sitting in the cafeteria was as quiet as a church, listening to the entire song. "Oh, that was beautiful," said Riya. "We're going to build a perfect world," said Mike.

At 9:00, we had sent out the remaining specialists so that each group would have a leader. Linda had shuffled the participants to avoid any groupings by nationality or religious background. I didn't want such thinking to exist, though, of course, I wouldn't interfere with anyone's religious beliefs. That was a personal matter. Personally, I'd been more or less atheist my whole life. And now, with 12 billion people having died on Earth in a very painful way, it was hard for me to believe that there could be a good god standing there, handing out tickets to heaven and hell. In my view, such a god would be very sadistic if not perverse in its thinking. But sometimes, I envied those who believed and could find comfort in prayer or similar practices. And there's nothing wrong with gaining mental strength.

Another issue was language. All participants spoke fluent English, but we represented over 100 nationalities. If we take the three Swedes among us as an example, should we encourage them to teach their children Swedish? Or would they speak both English and Swedish? I wanted the participants to think about questions like this.

I hadn't taken a group for myself but instead floated among the groups, answering questions and perhaps giving my perspective. But the enthusiasm in the groups was fantastic. One question that came up a few times was whether there would be a church, mosque, synagogue, temple, or something similar. I said we'd try to build a meditation room where people could go to pray or just socialize, for those who wished. But there would be no segregation or idolization; we were all the same people. In this room, Jews, Muslims, different Christian denominations, Buddhists, Hindus, or anyone else could gather and find peace. Now we had the chance to do things differently. I would consider it a nightmare scenario if people started dividing themselves by religion and part of our little village became sectioned off by religious areas. Nothing good had ever come from that on Earth, not to mention the millions of lives lost because of differing beliefs about the afterlife. Religious fundamentalists had indeed been screened out early in the selection process.

I went over to see how Jose and the others were getting started. As I guessed, they were seated in groups according to their areas of expertise, sketching and talking enthusiastically. One thing they all had in common: everyone had access to Linda and used her constantly. "Boss, come over here and take a look," called Jose. "We may have found our new home," he laughed. The entire group gathered to watch as Jose showed the screen: "Lake Bolgoda, the largest lake in Sri Lanka, flows out into the Indian Ocean. The agronomists are already considering the first rice harvest. We can get fresh water from there for all our needs. The entire west coast is quite developed, so finding building materials won't be a problem. It would be a simple solution at first, and we could get the infrastructure up and running relatively quickly. The sanitation group has made good progress as well as the road builders."

"How far would it be between our villages?" I asked.

"Only 30 km. I know you wanted more distance, but this could simplify communication and allow us to help each other more quickly. Plus, there's an old railway running along the coast. Imagine if we could get it working again and fix up a handcart for transporting goods between the villages, even with a manually operated transport vehicle."

"And you've done all this in an hour?" I asked.

"Yes," Jose answered, smiling.

"What can I say? Fantastic job. Tonight, you'll present your plans to everyone, and then we'll hold a little celebration afterward." We all applauded each other, and everyone dove back into the maps and continued planning. What a team, what a darn good team.

Celebration, well, it was alcohol-free, but everyone could eat their fill with our substitutes and dream about our new home. The enthusiasm was contagious. Everyone buzzed around and mingled with each other. Josh started by presenting his plans and was interrupted by applause and cheers at regular intervals. Later, everyone was talking over each other with excitement. Ra wandered around and made sure no one felt left out. Mike did much the same. And, as I somewhat expected, Mike and Ra seemed to get along very well.

"How long do you think it'll be before they announce they're together?" Riya asked.

"My guess is two hours until they're together, and by tomorrow, they'll announce it," I replied. Riya, the romantic, guessed that they'd be together in a week and announce it afterward. But I won.

The days went by quickly, and everyone was eager for something to do. Many trained outside of Linda's program, working on their own routines. We had a well-equipped gym, and it was full all the time. I stuck with Linda's program, trusting her. Besides, I wanted a little more time with Riya every day, which was entirely new for me compared to my previous relationships.

I had also asked everyone to read William Golding's book *Lord of the Flies*. The book is about a group of boys aged 6–12 who are shipwrecked after a plane crash. At first, everything goes well, but then they start to split into groups, and conflicts arise between the former friends. It ends in anarchy, and even a young boy is accidentally killed. My intention wasn't to "paint a bleak picture" but rather to give everyone an understanding that things can go wrong. I was now convinced that my community council policy would work initially, although there was a risk that they'd rely too heavily on me, Riya, and the other leaders. And, of course, we were directly dependent on their expertise in various fields at the start. We would also find out everyone's interests and what might interest them. We needed a workforce, though no one was forced to work, but I believed everyone understood that it was in all our interests to contribute.

I also thought about how we could keep bureaucracy at bay. I believed that the best approach would be to have no secrets – everyone should know exactly how much food, supplies, and medicine were available for everyone. No one would have any privileges; everyone would help build the houses in the village. It was certainly most important that everyone would have their own home. Simple and small at first, and if anyone wanted to expand later, that would be their choice. Hopefully, the houses would get bigger over time, if things went as we hoped, and the baby boom would begin. I was convinced that everything would work out – blood, sweat, and tears, for sure, but hopefully, happy tears as well.

Time flew by, and now it was only eight days until the next sedation, and naturally, everyone was nervous, remembering what had happened with Susan Hallenberg. Everyone followed Linda's instructions precisely.

One morning, after breakfast, Mike stood up and said, "Hey, I just wanted to share some news: Ra and I are together." Sakari shouted, "Okay, and what's the news?" Everyone burst into laughter but gave the couple a big round of applause. Riya went over to Ra and hugged her. "See, everyone likes you."

"John, I hope Ra and I can be in the same group."

"What do you mean? It's only 30 km between the villages; you can run that in no time. Of course, buddy – you're both in the same group with me and Riya." Mike hugged me so hard I thought my ribs would break. Linda played David Bowie's *Starman* for Mike. I'd almost become like a DJ; people enjoyed my old classic taste. "He's a starman, waiting in the sky..." everyone belted out in the chorus.

18. THE RESERVS

When there were only a few days left, a rather surprising incident occurred. I was sitting in my room with Riya, Mike, and Ra when a participant, whom I remembered as one of those who joined at the last minute – one of the so-called "reserves" – knocked on the door. "Hello, sorry to disturb," said a young man named Rocco Torro from Estonia. I remembered him because of his unique name. "Yes, we reserves have gathered in the cafeteria and would like to speak with you," he said, nodding toward me. "Okay, I'll be there in 5 minutes." I had an inkling of what they wanted, so I said, "Riya and Mike, wait here, but Ra, may I take you with me?" "Of course, Captain," she replied. "But Ra, if it's okay with you, I'll be a bit tough on you in the cafeteria. Can you handle that?" I asked. "You don't know what that means, Captain," she laughed.

The so-called reserves, all 40 of them, were seated in the cafeteria. Rocco Torro spoke up. "Yes, we've talked about this, and we feel a bit left out. I mean, we took spots from people who didn't make it when the war broke out. Now we feel maybe a bit inferior to those who were chosen directly, and there's some guilt toward those who were left behind. It's almost like the others are in the A-team and we're in the B-team." I sat quietly for a moment, looking them in the eye. Then I stood up. "The B-team, huh? Linda, play the application I asked for earlier."

I had previously asked Linda to play Ra's application without the video in the room. "Hey there, forest fogeys. I'm from Ireland and have only been chipped for a year. I don't have any education to brag about, but I'm good at surviving. I learned to read from cookie packages, and an old man taught me numbers so I'd know how old things were. If we run into trouble with aliens or other space crap, I'll fix it with my knife. I have no idea where you're headed, but if you want a loyal participant who can handle anything, take me along. That's all. Hope someone reads the message."

"Out of thousands of applications, this one stood out. All the other applications were very formal, like a job interview, and they were mostly indistinguishable from each other. So everyone who came along was lucky – not just those chosen directly, not just the reserves. Some were unlucky, like those who didn't make it. There was nothing we could do about it. We were in a hurry, and as we know, we almost lost the last rocket. So, there is no B-team. And what team would you place the application we just listened to?"

A woman, Annabella Ross from the U.S., raised her hand. "C," she said, and most chuckled along with her. "As I said, I never saw the application, but fortunately, Mike did. Could the woman with the voice please stand up?" Ra stood up. "Ra!" everyone exclaimed. "Sorry, Ra," said Annabella. "I didn't mean anything by it." "It's alright, kiddo," Ra replied.

"But the point I wanted to make, I think, got across: everyone is equally important. And if anyone has a different opinion, they can come and talk to me about it. And if that doesn't work, I'll send Ra." Appreciative laughter and applause followed, and a few, including Annabella, went over to hug Ra.

"But since you're all here, I'll continue for a bit. We have people from many different cultures, which is a central part of the entire project – diversity. And now, more than ever, remember that no one is better than anyone else, no culture or religion is superior or 'correct.' There may be slight nuances in religions, but in the big picture, they all have the same essence. Personally, I've chosen a safer or easier path by being an atheist. But I equally respect those who wish to be religious. We are all different, and I see that as an enormous asset. We are going to live together in peace for generations, so I hope we can find a common path. Are we in agreement on that?" Everyone agreed, and I walked back to the room with Ra. She took my hand and skipped beside me like Little Red Riding Hood again. I took a few skips as well.

"We followed the discussion from here on the screen," Mike said. "I'm so proud of you," he said, giving Ra a kiss on the lips. "And as for the Captain, he put them in their place," Ra laughed. "Well, it wasn't really about that, just a simple example. Also, to show that sometimes things shouldn't be overthought or are just as they are. Salespeople have a saying: 'KISS' – keep it simple, stupid."

Riya continued, "It's been a long wait, and everyone has stayed healthy, so we're on schedule. But tomorrow is vaccination day as a preventive measure, just in case any trace of the pandemic remains, though I don't think it does. The reason we take the vaccine before sedation is that, essentially, the body remains inactive during that time, so it has a couple of days to take effect here and a couple of days while we're asleep."

"What happens if a new epidemic breaks out?" wondered Ra. "I find it unlikely," replied Riya. "Major epidemics usually arise due to poor hygiene, possibly from overpopulation or similar factors, and we don't have that risk. But the best thing we can do is quickly get sanitation in order. There are other risks too, like rabies, so we have to be cautious with animals. And if we hunt anything, we can test the meat before we eat it – there are parasites like trichinella in pigs and wild boars as well. But in our first years, we have a good supply of medicines and various vaccines. Hopefully, we'll be able to produce more in the future. I have full confidence that everything will go well on that front. Furthermore, I hope lots of babies will be born; maybe Mike and Ra will be the first," Riya laughed.

"I bet the Captain and the lady will beat us to it, with all the time you spend in your room," Ra retorted. "Well, you never know what might happen, but no one can be pregnant during sedation. That would be outright dangerous," Riya replied. "But as pleasant as this is, tomorrow will be another busy day," I said. "And I promised to read Riya a bedtime story, so we'll continue tomorrow."

"Can you read me a bedtime story too, Ra?" asked Mike. "I usually do, don't I?" Ra answered with a wink.

After breakfast, the medical team began the vaccinations, and you could see how experienced they all were. It didn't take long before everyone was protected against what was hopefully an already extinct disease. Better safe than sorry. The rest of the day, we took it easy and talked with the participants. Everyone seemed much calmer than before the first sedation. People asked questions that no one could truly answer, as we didn't know what the world would look like. Personally, I went around dreaming of fresh fruit, completely fed up with all the substitute stuff we'd been stuffing ourselves with. But one had to be grateful for what was available. Yet, the thought of pineapple, coconut milk, and mango made my mouth water.

"What are you dreaming about again?" asked Riya. "Fresh fruit," I answered honestly. "Not such big dreams, John." "What do you dream of, Mrs. Carter? How can I complete your life?" "A small house with an ocean view, where we can grow old together with our daughter." "If we'd stayed on Earth, that would have been nearly impossible to promise, but a house with an ocean view we can manage, and fate will take care of the rest. We could even build a summer cabin in the jungle overlooking wild elephants and other animals." "That sounds wonderful, John. Have you thought about the wildlife? I mean, the populations have probably strengthened, even though nature has its way of keeping it in balance. But there were also a lot of zoos with exotic animals – tigers, lions, gorillas, and so on. If I'd worked at a zoo, I would have let the animals free when things went south. And then there are all the domesticated animals – chickens, pigs, donkeys, horses, cows – there could be anything out there."

"Not really," I admitted. "I should probably talk to Sakari about this if we need to take any measures. But he doesn't know what it looks like either. But we have weapons to protect ourselves if needed, and perhaps we'll need some sort of fence or protection for our crops too. I think I'll go talk to Sakari right now and that agronomist from Bangladesh with the unusual name." "You mean Jhumpa Banik?" Riya laughed. "That's the one," I chuckled.

Sakari and Jhumpa had already thought it through. Electric fencing – the simplest solution. A lightly electrified fence would deliver a harmless shock but enough to keep animals away. "How much of it do we have?" I asked. "Enough for several kilometers if we just make one loop around; it'll keep antelope and similar animals out," replied Jhumpa Banik. "But if a herd of elephants ran wild, there's nothing we could do to stop them," Sakari added. "But we can't start shooting elephants," I objected. "That's definitely a last resort. We'll think about it – loud noises could scare them off, maybe fire as well," Sakari replied.

"But don't worry about it now; you've got plenty of other things to focus on. We'll handle it as it comes once we've marked out the fields. Just get us down to Earth, John, and we'll take care of this," said Jhumpa.

"You're right; why should someone like me meddle in everything? I mean, you're the experts here." "Just normal curiosity, I suppose. And the more people are engaged in the projects, the better. We have lots of enthusiastic young people in all areas. We'll take them as apprentices and necessary labor. Hunting, fishing, farming – with those, we'll secure our sustenance. And was it you who said it? We're heading into the Stone Age with modern technology. We have every chance to start life as a dream," said Sakari.

"I think it was Riya who said it, but that's what we're aiming for. Thank you," I concluded.

Later, we snuck away with a glass of my Chivas Regal each, sitting on a couch together in silence, looking out the window with Riya. Everything was dark, and in the infinity, we saw what were likely stars, suns, planets – who knows. How could it be like this? How could it be so vast? And there I sat, feeling content. I think Riya felt the same when she took my hand and leaned against me. As far as I was concerned, life could have paused right there and in that place. But we had to move forward – such is human nature: curious, inventive, and restless. It had always been that way, and perhaps it always would be.

19.
GOODNIGHT AGAIN

The day finally came, the one most people had been waiting for, some with a bit of fear and worry. We all remembered Susan Hallenberg's passing. I, however, pushed aside the thought that something similar could happen again. Sure, the odds were somewhat against us, as we'd been warned that, on average, one in a thousand might not wake up. But I had a feeling that we'd beat the odds this time.

Many couples had already formed among the participants, which pleased me. We hadn't yet done the group division for that very reason; we didn't know exactly who was with whom or who was interested in whom. Admittedly, it would be much easier to stay in contact between groups since the distance would only be around 30 km. So, it wouldn't be a disaster if someone unintentionally ended up in the wrong group. But after waking up, we'd have to sort that out with Linda's help.

We decided not to prolong the sedation process. The longer people were left idle, the more anxious they'd become. We used the same approach as last time. The specialists got a group selected by Linda on the screen, but this time we skipped the "calming" drink, as everyone had realized it didn't have any effect. Everything went smoothly again. "See you soon," was the most common phrase people shouted to each other as they lay down in their capsules.

In the end, Riya and I stood there again, looking over the "capsule hall," hoping everyone's sleep would end well. "It feels so bittersweet again, Riya, though I know it feels like time will pass faster than when I'm waiting for you to finish brushing your teeth at night." "I know. I feel sad even though I'm standing right here next to you and will see you again in a moment." We hugged each other tightly, kissed, and decided it was best to just get it over with. Thoughts swirled in my head about what would happen if Riya didn't wake up. I tried to push those thoughts away. I didn't know how I'd handle the situation without her. I think Riya was on a similar wavelength, as her eyes shone as if she was close to shedding a tear. "Let's go now. See you soon." I gave Riya one last kiss and lay down in the capsule. The hatch closed quickly.

"Good morning, love." I smiled broadly at her. "That's the nicest thing I've ever heard in my life." I sat up in the capsule and downed the same drink as before – not that I had a headache this time, or maybe the euphoria just pushed it away. "Damn, Riya, we've slept for 400 years during the journey, and you're more beautiful than ever." "The privilege of waking up first – I got time to freshen up at my own pace," Riya laughed. "Go and shower in peace, and I'll start waking people up. We have vital signs from all the capsules." "Wonderful, I'll be there soon to help you."

The room looked exactly the same as it did 200 years ago. "Hey, Linda, did you miss me?" "I know how I'm supposed to answer if that's what you mean." "That's exactly what I mean," I laughed. "Pleasure to have you back, John." "Nice to hear you too, but now you've got work to do. Shower, 37 degrees." The water came immediately. "Shall we listen to some music, Linda?" "What would you like to hear?" "'Wunderbar' by Ten Pole Tudor," and turn up the volume. The sound boomed in the shower, and I roared along with the chorus, "Wunderbar, Wunderbar," and that's exactly how it felt – life was just perfect now. Best to just enjoy it, and I was sure I'd miss this shower.

Riya had already woken up about 20 people, and the pace would pick up as more people finished their showers and started helping with the drinks. "Wunderbar, wunderbar," sang Riya, laughing. I realized I must've been singing a bit loud in the shower and apologized. Riya just laughed, "You should've heard me back then." "What did you sing?" I asked as I handed a drink to a participant. "I'm not telling you." "But I told you." "No, I heard you – that's a big difference." "I think that's cheating; next time, I'm waking up first." "There won't be a next time," Riya replied. "It's nice to have it over with; not everything went according to plan, but I feel like we made the right choices." "You did everything perfectly, John, everything."

We let everyone recover a bit and come for the surrogate food, which was now 200 years older but tasted the same. "Pineapple" swirled in my head again. A few more days here, and then with the shuttles down to Earth. There was a lot to prepare, but luckily, Linda was there. I was the one who decided who could use it. I had given Riya full access, and she could delegate Linda to whomever she wanted. But sometimes, everyone had the right to use Linda at the same time; she had the capacity, so that wasn't a problem.

We sat down with Riya, Mike, Ra, Jose, Sakari, and Yong and pondered the lists. We decided that in Group One, with me, Riya, Mike, and Ra, there would be 392 women and 390 men. In Group Two, led by Jose, Sakari, and Yong, there would be 391 women and 389 men. I asked them to figure out how to make the distribution of specialists as even as possible. It was considerably trickier to ensure gender balance. Sometimes, one group would end up with more healthcare personnel, while the other had more agronomists. But still, both groups had sufficient numbers.

We then decided that Linda would create the groupings on the screen. She also knew, via the chip, who was paired up, and so on. For example, separating the four Japanese participants into different groups wasn't even a consideration. Later in the day, they could swap places as long as the gender distribution remained balanced. By the end of the day, the groups were ready, and everyone seemed satisfied. Everywhere you went, you could sense excitement and anticipation.

Banil Mandara, who was from Sri Lanka, was the one who was asked the most questions. I asked him to tell us a bit about what we could expect when we arrived. "Hello, my name is Banil Mandara, and I'm from Sri Lanka. Actually, the university I studied at is not far from where we're headed. I'm from Jaffna in northern Sri Lanka. It's February now, so it's very warm, though it's like that all year round. You'll probably never feel cold again, with temperatures ranging from 25°C to 33°C year-round. In April, the rainy season begins, so we'll need a roof over our heads. It rains from April to June and again from September to November. The biggest danger in Sri Lanka is the sun, so protect your head when you're outside, and be aware of how easily you can get sunburned. The jungle has likely taken over, so there will be many buildings, but don't go into them, and don't move around alone. Stray dogs were once an issue in Colombo and may have multiplied; they can be very aggressive when protecting their territories – unless, of course, the tigers have eaten them."

There was a murmur in the audience. "There are actually no tigers in Sri Lanka – there used to be only in zoos or possibly with private owners. But now we don't know what happened to the animals in the zoos. Were they put down, released, or did they adapt to a new environment, and so on? There were a few wild leopards, but all big cats are shy of humans. They'll leave us alone as long as we don't disturb them. There are also many wild elephants, as well as domesticated ones, so they could pose a problem as well." "What about snakes?" someone asked. "There are quite a few snakes, but snakes are usually harmless if they have a chance to escape, which they usually take. Most people who were bitten by snakes had confronted them. So, leave them alone, and they won't bother you. It wasn't my intention to scare you; Sri Lanka is a fantastic country with the best climate in the world, fertile land, and dream beaches. We're going to have a wonderful life together. Thank you."

Banil received a resounding round of applause and was approached throughout the day. Patiently, he answered everyone's questions. A great guy.

I got a chance to sit down with Ra when she took a little break from her duties. If she didn't have any, she would make sure to help wherever she could. "How's it going, Ra?" "Full throttle, Captain, full throttle." "That's what I wanted to talk about a bit." "Is there a problem?" she asked immediately. "No, quite the opposite, Ra. We all love you just as you are. I just don't want you to burn yourself out. You don't need to prove anything; you've already done more than enough. I know it's hard for you to trust people – I mean, you trust me and Riya and Mike, of course. But try to find friends for yourself, too. I think you'll see that the world isn't so evil. And believe me, I've seen a lot of darkness in my life working in corrections. But deep down, I believe in human goodness – it just has to be that way."

"Sorry," Ra said, "but after my security job, this is the only job I've ever had. And as a guard, my job was to knock people down along with the other guards – everyone who wasn't chipped who tried to storm into the store, we would knock down. That's how I finally got a chip myself, so I wouldn't get knocked down by mistake. I guess I was good at it, because I got one," she laughed. "As payment, we got food that had expired in the store and couldn't be sold to the chipped ones." "Remember that down on Earth, we're all just participants; we're all equal. And if everyone helps each other, we'll have a good life. Tomorrow, we're in Sri Lanka, Ra."

"Can you teach me to swim, Captain?" "I'll do that, I promise," I laughed. "You're the best, Captain," Ra said and gave me a big hug.

20. BENTOTA, BALAPITIYA

After thorough studies with the agronomists, fishers, and hunters, they had arrived at the following results with Linda's help. Yong presented the planning to the specialists and everyone interested in listening. And that meant everyone on board. So she used the speaker so everyone could hear on the screens, as there wasn't enough space in the cafeteria.

"Yes, hello," Yong began. "We've now thought this through carefully, and with Linda's help, we've come to the following conclusions. The locations will be Bentota, which is on the west coast and has beautiful, long, sandy beaches. But the most important thing – even though the beach is important – is that we have access to Lake Balgoda for freshwater, both for ourselves and for farming. The other location is called Balapitiya, near Migettuwaththa Beach, where we have access to freshwater from the Madu River. To simplify the names, we've called them Bentota and Madu; otherwise, only Banil can pronounce them. And as you know, the shuttles have only one chance to land; once we're down, they'll stay there for good. The shuttles function as hospitals, and we can also spend the night there at first if the jungle scares you. Does that sound good?" The applause answered that question.

I said, "Stay up there so people can ask questions." "Hi, my name is Nina. I wonder how far it will be between the locations, and if we'll have the chance to meet each other." It was unmistakable – she was Italian. Yong replied, "With John's blessing, we're allowed to be close to each other, probably no more than 10 kilometers as the crow flies. But we shouldn't forget that it could be quite overgrown. However, I think, with everyone's help, we'll soon have a jungle path ready. So we'll definitely be able to have a beach party in the near future."

I asked to speak. "Four hundred years is a very long time, but I believe and hope that we'll arrive at a tropical paradise that, with our collective will, will work perfectly. We all help each other, and we understand that everything we do is for our own good. My hope is that we get to breathe clean air, swim in turquoise water, and build families where everyone supports each other. No one has a nicer car, more money, better clothes, or more food. Now it's just us, and we are few, and we are the last. But now we have preparations, so we'll keep it short. Tomorrow morning, we'll be going down to Earth."

The grouping was nearly complete; some people wanted to switch places, which worked out as it fulfilled the gender quota. We decided that Group 1 would go to Bentota and Group 2 to Madu. We'd inspected the fairly large shuttles and confirmed that there was plenty of space now that we had two available. We began unloading *Quasitor* with whatever might be needed, including all the surrogate provisions. I hoped I'd get my pineapple soon and wouldn't have to touch that damn sludge anymore. Even though *Quasitor* would remain in Earth's orbit, it might take thousands of years before Linda would receive visitors again. It was almost sad to think of her alone – she'd become so important to us.

I realized that the world I was trying to build was very similar to the vision of the philosopher John Lennon. In his time, it wasn't possible, so it was probably just a dream for him – a time they called the hippie era. Back then, they rattled nuclear weapons and used them to intimidate, but those became obsolete once they installed space-based laser cannons that could destroy them seconds after launch. If any country had tried it, they'd only have shot themselves in the foot, as they'd detonate on their own soil. Eventually, the weapons were dismantled.

After that, there was more capacity to develop nuclear technology, both for energy supply and space technology. For a while, things looked pretty good in the civilized world. At least for those who were chipped – they had blinders on and wax in their ears. They continued to support poor countries with food and money that ended up in the wrong hands. And it didn't take long before the masses from the south started moving. The elite lived in their own bubble and couldn't handle the invasion. So here we were now, the elite snobs and Ra.

Riya and I were lying in bed, talking. "Hard to believe it's our last night in space. When do you think the next person will come up here, John?" "I think it will happen someday. Humanity is naturally curious and inventive. It won't be in our lifetime, but maybe our daughter will become an astronaut someday, who knows?" "She won't be an astronaut; she'll be a pearl diver so she can bring beautiful pearls for her mom," Riya replied. "I like it when you say Mom; do you want to be one?" "I think all women do, but first, I want that house with the ocean view you promised." "But we can still practice for that in the meantime," I said. "A little practice never hurts," Riya laughed.

Linda had finalized the departure times. Group 2 would leave at 09:45, with Group 1 following just 15 minutes later. Craig had mentioned earlier that he would "go down with the sinking ship," like people did in the old days. Maybe that's why Linda chose for Group 1 to start later. Either way, 15 minutes didn't make a difference overall. Riya had insisted that everyone clean their rooms perfectly – likely a habit from her military days. She explained that we were leaving a piece of history behind. It would be nice if, when someone next visited *Quasitor* in a few thousand years, they would see that their ancestors were tidy people. But everyone was eager for something to do, so this task fit in well.

Additionally, Riya wanted everyone to write a welcome message and sign their names. I thought it was a nice gesture, so I wrote, "I lived on *Quasitor* for 400 years, of which I slept through all but one month. Take good care of Linda, and ask her to tell you about me. Fly well, best wishes, John Carter."

We all gathered when Group 1 marched in orderly fashion into the shuttle. Everything was computer-controlled, and once again, we entrusted ourselves entirely to the fate of technology. But we had done that so far, and everything had worked perfectly, so we continued to trust it. What choice did we have if something went wrong? No one had any training in space technology. Ra thought she'd take control of the levers if there was an issue. I didn't doubt that for a second.

We didn't have time for lengthy farewells between the groups, as it was already our turn to board the shuttle. The pigs had been loaded earlier; about 8% of them hadn't survived the sedation and were unceremoniously sent off on an adventure in space. I wondered what some civilization would think if they encountered our dead pigs floating through space. The survivors looked lively and healthy and had curiously entered their stalls, separated from us. They had then been secured due to gravity and other factors. But they were hardy animals and would probably manage the journey. The thousands of fertilized chicken eggs were, of course, with us. Setting up the animal enclosures was our first priority, but our specialists already had clear plans. They had to be relatively close to us so we could protect them from, for example, wild animals.

We were strapped into the shuttle and heard the roar of the first shuttle as it took off. Riya and I held each other's hands, and I noticed that Mike and Ra were doing the same. Many others, too, which was nice to see. Tense expressions were everywhere, but if all went well, we might all be swimming in the Indian Ocean within a few hours.

"What do you think it looks like down there?" Riya asked. "Your guess is probably as good as mine – overgrown, warm, and we'll have to be very cautious at first."

"What worries me the most, with us being close to freshwater, are the mosquitoes. We have medicine for malaria, luckily, but dengue, yellow fever, Zika virus, etc., are things we'll need to watch out for. Everyone must use mosquito repellent in the evenings. But everyone's well-informed, so I think we'll manage."

"Nice to have a wife who's a doctor," I replied.

Then we heard the detachment and the engines starting up. I felt completely helpless. "Here am I sitting in a tin can," I hummed David Bowie's *Space Oddity*. And that's exactly how I felt. After a bumpy ride with a lot of G-forces, things began to lighten up, and everyone looked out the windows. But it was still too early to see Earth; white clouds still separated us. Then suddenly, the clouds cleared, and we saw Earth. We all cheered, leaning in eagerly to get a better view.

"We're above India, my home!" Riya shouted. Everyone cheered and applauded as we flew over southern India toward Sri Lanka. "When we see the sea, we're close." Riya was shaking; I could see she was excited, happy, and tense. "Oh, John," she said and kissed me. The screen showed we were flying over a place on India's west coast called Pattanamarudur. Now we could clearly see the beach, palm trees, and sand. I didn't have time to see any buildings before we were already out over the sea, turquoise as I'd hoped. But there was no sign of life, no boats. The screen showed we'd land in Bentota in 20 minutes. The shuttle would circle a bit, looking for a flat enough spot to land. Again, nothing we could do; everything was automatic. Maybe it would be the last time we'd all be completely helpless. We were now very close to descending; we caught a glimpse of the beach, which looked endless, but we were too excited to take much note of it. The shuttle barely moved, slowly descending, and then suddenly, we were down. The engines went silent at the same time. I said over the speakers, "Welcome home." The cheers were endless as people jumped, shouted, and hugged each other.

"You're welcome to stay seated if you want, but I'm planning on taking a dip in the sea – anyone coming?" "Yesss!" was the answer. I stayed back and let the others rush off; nothing would have stopped them. "Now, off with those embarrassing underwear," Riya said, handing me a T-shirt, shorts, and sunglasses from my personal pack. "Wonderful," I replied. "Leave them here and go down to the beach with the others. I need to check in with Jose and make sure everything's okay."

Jose answered immediately, "Hi, all good here. The landing went well, and everyone rushed to the beach. The only issue is a large troop of monkeys – probably about 200. Sakari shot at the most aggressive ones, and they've retreated now. Hopefully, they understood to keep their distance. But no one got bitten. How about you?"

"Haven't made it out yet, but everyone else rushed to the beach here too. The journey and landing went well. I hope we get a moment to breathe, but that's probably wishful thinking." "Yeah, here they're busy putting up a shelter for the pigs, full speed ahead." "Glad to hear everything went well; let's touch base later. I'm going to check out our new home."

I quickly changed and looked like a proper beach tourist. I stepped out of the shuttle and used the chip to close the door. It felt like a wet dishcloth had been thrown in my face – humid and warm. About 300 meters away, I saw the others splashing around in the water. All around me, I could only hear insects and birds, loads of birds. But no monkeys in sight.

Then I suddenly froze – a massive water buffalo was standing and staring at me from 50 meters away. I didn't dare move; damn. I didn't feel like Tarzan anymore. I'd heard they could be dangerous if they felt threatened. I wanted to run to the beach but didn't know how it would react. But how would I warn the group if I went back to the shuttle? I asked for the door to open anyway and slowly walked closer to it. I thought that if I shouted and made noise, it might retreat, but I couldn't get too close. I shouted and waved my arms, taking a few steps toward it.

It slowly turned and walked into the vegetation. Maybe I had some Tarzan genes after all.

I gathered my courage and walked briskly toward the others, glancing back constantly.

Down at the beach, I went over to a hunter – I remembered his name as Jack Barker, an Englishman. I told him what I'd seen. "I'll take a couple of the hunting team with me and check it out. It's probably a water buffalo descended from domesticated animals. There was once a wild water buffalo species, but I believe it went extinct. However, these domesticated ones have been used in agriculture for thousands of years. They're wild now, but maybe we could catch and tame a few," Jack mused.

"Sounds like a good idea, but let's take it slow at first. It's good to scout the area and see what's around," I replied. "Now, I'm going for a swim." I saw Riya, Mike, and Ra standing waist-deep in the water. I ran over to them; the water felt fantastic and was crystal clear. I wrapped one arm around Riya's waist.

"How's it going over at Madu?" Mike asked. "They're doing well; most of them are swimming. They initially had a bit of a problem with aggressive monkeys – a troop of a couple of hundred, and they shot at the most aggressive ones. They retreated, and hopefully, they'll keep their distance. We're intruding on their territory, but we don't have much choice. We'll have to learn to coexist with the animals. Meanwhile, we have water buffalo nearby. Jack is going to check things out with some help."

Riya said, "An exciting start." "No worries; you have Tarzan here," I said, beating my chest. "And Ra," Mike added, only to be immediately knocked over into the water by Ra.

21. CLEARING

After an hour or so of relaxation, you could sense that everyone was eager to start doing something meaningful. People started gathering around Riya and me as we sat in the shade of a palm tree. "Are you all getting keen to get to work?" I asked. Everyone nodded eagerly. "I promise you can work as much as you like, but you're also free to take a break if needed. But remember, everything we do here, we do for each other. Our thought was this: the most urgent thing now is to set up shelter for the night, and Jack here has experience with that. So, those who want to build wind shelters and gather materials for it, please follow Jack." A large group went with him.

"Then, we need supplies from the shuttle, so a few of you can go fetch some food, fire-starters, and such," Ra volunteered to take care of it. "But be careful if you see any of those water buffalo I mentioned. They'll probably retreat, but you never know. Mike needs a few helpers to set up an 'outhouse,' and please place it a bit away, thanks. So, a few strong folks who don't mind sweating and digging."

"We'll also need plenty of help for the agronomists and road builders. As you can see, we're surrounded by thick jungle, so we need to clear some space for moving around besides just the beach. Jack might need roof materials for the shelters. There are lots of abandoned buildings around, but don't go inside them. We have a lifetime to explore those. Right now, we need food and a place to sleep quickly. If anyone prefers, you can sleep on the shuttle's floor space, but ideally, we'd like the doctors to set up their clinic there. Tools like shovels, machetes, knives, and other essentials are on the shuttle."

Everyone started moving, almost running, eager to get to work. It looked promising. "I'll go to the shuttle – I imagine it won't be long before we have some patients there with cuts and blisters on their hands." I could see that Riya was excited about setting up her little clinic and starting to care for people.

I heard they'd gotten our electric tractor running, so I went over to see what they were up to. About two hundred meters south, a bit into the vegetation, I saw them gathered around the tractor. "We have a gift for you, John," the female excavator operator shouted. She held out a small pineapple to me. "Oh, I've been dreaming of this! But is it ripe? It's pretty small." "It's a smaller variety – much sweeter and juicier. We've already eaten a few. There are plenty in there."

Mike pulled out a familiar hunting knife and cut it into four slices. I gratefully accepted one and bit into it. It was indescribably delicious – the juice just ran down my cheeks. "Thank you; this is the best thing I've ever eaten. Pick more so we can have some for dinner. Pineapple with surrogate food might not be so bad after all. By the way, how are you handling the outhouse?" I asked.

"How about a flush toilet?" Banil asked with his usual smile. "How do you mean?" I asked. "We found a side stream off the river. Susan in the excavator thinks she can divert the water here, so it flows under you while you're doing your business, and then we'll dig it so it drains into the ocean a bit south of here. The sea currents will take care of it from there." "That's brilliant! This was something I was worried about – it could get pretty unpleasant in this heat otherwise."

We heard a few gunshots, and I left the group, heading toward the sound. I saw the hunters hauling something as I got closer. "Hi," said Jack. "We took down four wild boars. There are plenty of them here. A veterinarian is on the way to check if the meat is safe to eat. We'll butcher them here and bury the innards. We need to drain the blood and prepare them quickly to avoid spoilage in the heat." "Well, then, a beach barbecue – with pineapple, too," I laughed.

As I walked toward the shuttle, I saw nearly 100 people hacking their way along what used to be a road. The first ones with machetes took turns every few minutes, while others behind them piled up the brush on the sides. You could already see patches of the old asphalt under the vegetation that hadn't yet deteriorated. A lot had happened in just a couple of hours, so I thought I'd take a look at the clinic.

Several of the road builders were there getting patched up for minor cuts from the vegetation. A young woman had cut her foot pretty badly, and I saw Riya skillfully stitch and bandage it. A guy lay on the floor with an ice pack on his head – probably too much sun.

When the solar panels eventually wore out after some years, we would only be able to dream of ice. How would we explain to our children what ice was? A child growing up in the tropics. I could almost hear the questions already: "Dad, what is ice? What does 'freeze' mean? What is 'cold'?" But I hoped our skilled team would find a solution.

We had only been here a few hours, and soon we'd have a flush toilet, the hospital was running smoothly, a beach barbecue was coming up, and we'd already made progress on the road. I wouldn't be surprised if the farming work was well underway, too. I waved to Riya, signaling that I'd continue on, not wanting to disturb her further.

About a hundred meters from the shuttle, I heard grunting and walked toward it. The pigs had a great start here in Bentota. Jhumpa explained to me, "We found an old building here and knocked down one of the walls so the pigs could use it as a feeding spot and shelter from the sun and rain. We put an electric fence around it, so don't touch it – the pigs learned quickly. The area is nearly 100 meters wide and 150 meters long, so they have plenty of space and seem to be thriving. And if you look over there, they're planting corn right now."

"That's amazing," I said. "I'm starting to feel like I have no role as a leader anymore – everything gets done instantly, and I'm just waiting around for the barbecue and pineapple." "You'll always be a leader in our eyes, for all of us here, regardless of what you do."

I went to check on the agronomists. They had cleared an area the size of a football field. There were a couple of hundred people altogether who had leveled the ground and dug a canal from the river to irrigate the field. And, as Jhumpa said, they were already sowing seeds. I spoke to a young man I recognized as the guy from Finland who was resting on a rock. "Hi, Joni, how are you feeling? It's been a busy day."

"Ever since this project began, it's felt like I've come home – it's amazing. All these people from different backgrounds, this place. It feels safe when everyone's so willing to help with everything. We're going to make this work, Captain." I didn't bother correcting him again. Apparently, I'd become 'Captain' whether I liked it or not, so I'd just have to get used to it. As long as Riya kept calling me John.

"I feel the same, Joni, but don't wear yourself out." "We have something in Finland we call *sisu*, a kind of euphoria that comes out when times are tough, and we give it everything we've got." "Sisu," I replied. "I'll remember that."

It was an incredible first evening on the beach. Four wild boars roasting on spits, along with pineapple and mango that had been found. Everyone ate their fill. A long line of wind shelters stretched along the beach – it seemed everyone wanted to sleep outside on the first night. Outside the shelters, many had lit fires and sat in groups, talking. Our line of shelters was likely 150-200 meters long. Riya and I walked hand in hand back and forth, talking with the participants. The day had been productive in many ways, and I guessed there would be major progress in the coming days.

In the distance, we heard dogs. Jack suggested we get some dogs of our own – maybe capture a few pregnant females and tame them. The dogs would protect us, as they're very territorial. It sounded like a good idea, so I gave it the go-ahead. It would also help us dispose of leftover food. Tonight, the dogs would have had a feast on the bones and what remained of the wild boars.

A group of 20 people came up and asked if they could take a day trip to Madu to see how things were there. I thought it sounded like a good idea but insisted they bring a tent and plan to stay a night or two. It was about a 15-kilometer walk along the beach. However, I required them to take a hunter along as protection against potentially aggressive animals on the way. Additionally, a medic would need to accompany them in case anyone was bitten by a snake. Since the universal serum became available, snakebite fatalities had dropped drastically, but it required having the serum within reach. "But if you can convince a hunter and a medic, you're welcome to go out and get some exercise. It's about a 15-kilometer walk, so you'll need to start early before it gets too hot. I'll check in with Jose before it happens. But it would be great if you could stay here for the next few days to help with the clearing work – every hand is needed on deck." *On deck* – damn, I shouldn't have said that. Riya immediately responded, "Aye aye, Captain John."

We shared our shelter with Ra and Mike. We lay there, chatting, gazing at the starry sky, and thinking about Linda and *Quasitor*. "Do you think Linda has feelings?" Ra wondered. "As I understood it, she wasn't programmed with artificial intelligence," said Mike. "But sometimes it felt like she knew exactly what you were going to ask or where to lead the conversation."

The first time Riya and I slept together, I asked her to play classical music, and Linda chose Linda Ronstadt's song "It's So Easy to Fall in Love," I added. "That's sweet," Ra laughed. I noticed Riya had fallen asleep on my chest, so I gently moved her and said goodnight. "Goodnight, Captain, and thanks for today," replied Mike. I put my arm around Riya and fell asleep almost immediately, smiling.

22. A MONTH LATER

A lot had happened over the past 30 days. We had cleared the area, and it was beginning to look like a small village. We had uncovered the houses in a larger area as well. They were, of course, completely overgrown and very hard to access. Most of the roofs had collapsed, so we cleared out all the debris, leaving the walls as they were, and let the construction team assess whether they could build on them or if they needed to be demolished. We now had a significant amount of bricks that we organized in an open area for reuse, as well as roofing sheets that hadn't fully rusted through. In fact, we saved anything that could be repurposed. Many of the houses had already been restored enough for people to move into if they wanted. Surprisingly, the structures of the houses had held up well; most were built of concrete to resist termites, which devoured anything made of wood.

The sanitation engineers had designed a purification plant, and there was a lot of digging going on there. So far, our electric excavator tractor was holding up. We had spare parts for a while, but it ran almost constantly, so once it became unusable, progress would slow down.

One day, as I was helping clear out an area and walked behind a house, I spotted what I'd been looking for on a small hill nearby. It was the foundation of a small, almost completely collapsed house. But the location was just what Riya had dreamed of – a little house with an ocean view. "This is where I'd like my house," I said to Joni, who was with me. "Then take it," he replied instantly. "I don't want to be selfish and just claim something for myself, but the location is perfect. Look, there's a mango tree here too." I left it for the time being but thought I'd bring Riya here to take a look.

The next day, Riya and I went there, and I asked Joni to come along to make sure I'd find it again. A path had now been cleared to the spot, and I was a bit worried someone else might have had the same idea. But as we approached, I saw someone had engraved on a wooden plank: "Captain John and Riya Carter's residence." I looked at Joni, who shrugged and laughed, saying, "I may have mentioned to a few people that you liked the spot. Everyone agreed it was obvious you two should have it, and they all promised to come help whenever they had time."

"The location is amazing," Riya said, beaming like the sun. "And thank you, Joni." "We're the ones who are grateful to both of you. Everyone will do whatever they can for you."

Our house seemed to become a symbol of who we were and how our little community worked: kindness and helpfulness. Suddenly, there were at least 50 people working on the build, including sanitation engineers, carpenters, masons, and as many of the participants as could fit in the space. A little farther away, we found a larger building that had apparently been an aquarium for tourists at one time. It had a lot of plexiglass that had withstood the test of time. We used it as windows and partially for the roof, too, so we'd get natural light during the day.

The house turned out significantly larger than first planned, as Riya insisted that half of it function as a clinic where she could receive patients. A large terrace was cast at the back of the house with a beautiful ocean view. It eased my guilty conscience a bit to know that half of the house would serve as a clinic, so it wasn't just for our benefit. It became a duplex with two identical sides. Our side, where we'd live, had a living room upon entry and two bedrooms – one for us and one for our daughter, whom everyone was eagerly awaiting, even though she wasn't on the way yet. There was also a proper toilet, although it couldn't be used yet. Later, when the sanitation team got the purification plant running, it would be operational. A tower was also built to collect rainwater, which could then be used for the toilet and shower. There were plenty of toilet fixtures available, especially those with plastic mechanisms, many of which were still perfectly usable.

The other side of the house had a reception area and two smaller examination rooms, though for now, the shuttle served as the main hospital. The agronomists were making good progress too, and they estimated the corn they planted 30 days ago would have mature ears in another 30 days. Hundreds of chickens had also hatched and were being fed continuously, with no shortage of helpers. The pigs had grown considerably, and soon the veterinarians would begin fertilizing the first of them. Everything was progressing rapidly. Almost everyone was still sleeping on the beach, but I guessed that would change in another month.

The hunters had also captured three pregnant dogs. At first, they were kept in an enclosure, but they quickly began to trust us once they saw there was no danger and that they were well fed. They were free now, and everyone had grown accustomed to them; they often slept outside the shelters, curled up around the fire.

Time was moving under fortunate stars. We'd also had our first village meeting, where I served as village elder alongside 20 participants who would rotate every month. Their final task for the month would be to select a new village elder. I hoped they'd choose someone other than me – not because I was unwilling, but because the group needed to start stepping back from me and the other so-called leaders who'd held ranks on *Quasitor*. The meetings were very short and simple at first, as we mostly discussed the order of priorities for building houses, working the fields, hunting, fishing, and so on. Everything was progressing steadily, as everyone had meaningful work to do.

But one day, everything changed. We had seen smoke trickling up a few times deep in the jungle and had speculated about what it could be. A smoldering fire, a hot spring, etc. One morning, we decided, with Jack and Bandil, to take a hike closer to find out the source of the mysterious smoke. We started early in the morning; Riya was not at all on board with me going along. She said that, in that case, it would be better for her to go since she had jungle experience and a military background. But I calmed her down with "No worries, girl; it'll be nice to go on a little hike." And so it was. I almost regretted it after 15 minutes of hacking away with the machete; sweat was pouring, and the flies loved us. After a while, the terrain opened up, and after an hour, we had made good progress. Until we heard a "smack" on a tree next to us, and an arrow stuck out; we were surrounded by at least 20 people with bows drawn on us. We automatically raised our hands to show that we were unarmed, except for Jack, of course, who had a large rifle on his shoulder. But if he had made any move to use it, we would have been pierced by arrows instantly. And now comes the great fortune in this story: Bandil. Bandil was Tamil and spoke another language but could also speak Sinhalese, the majority language in Sri Lanka. First, he calmed them down enough that they lowered their bows slightly, though they were still on high alert. We sat down on the ground as a gesture that we didn't intend to attack or run away. After a while, they did the same. We (well, Bandil) started talking; our story was probably entirely utopian to them, but they told us they had seen us land in the "poisoned village," as they called it. They had stories handed down from their ancestors, who told of a disease that killed all sinful people, and a group of a few hundred had withdrawn to the jungle. Some among them were also sinful and had died. But the majority survived and now lived in the jungle. The atmosphere began to ease, and Bandil continued talking, translating for us. Someone brought out a long wooden pipe, lit it, and it went around so that everyone could take a puff. It would certainly have been impolite to decline, "marijuana," Jack whispered to me and took a big puff. I did the same and nearly choked in a fit of coughing. Apparently, this was funny, as everyone laughed, and after a while, I was laughing uncontrollably too. Why, I don't know. But I laughed until tears ran down my cheeks, which made everyone laugh even more. I was high for the first time in my life. We sat there for a good two hours, talking after we had calmed down and the high wore off somewhat. We shared our packed lunches, and they gave us some dried spiced fish to try. It actually became quite pleasant after a while. One of the locals pointed to Jack's rifle, and Jack explained that it was similar to their bow. They wanted Jack to demonstrate, so Jack fired a shot at a branch 50 meters away, which snapped off and fell to the ground. They were terrified by the bang, but their respect for Jack increased noticeably. Now they wanted us to follow them to their village. We didn't have much choice, so we followed. Luckily, there was a path, so the walk wasn't entirely impossible, even for me, who undoubtedly had the worst stamina of everyone. We walked a good 5 kilometers until we saw the smoke, which simply came from cooking fires. The whole village came out cautiously to meet us; small children hid behind their mothers. But the bravest came up and touched our white skin, mine and Jack's. The village was quite picturesque, with numerous huts built of stone and clay with thatched roofs. In the middle of it all was an open, square-like area with a well in the center. The village elder came toward us with open arms; his name was Raja, and he welcomed us but warned us against living in the "poisoned village." We told them we had medicine for the pandemic and could give them some if they wanted. They were, of course, a bit skeptical of our stories, but they figured that we couldn't be sinful since we could live there without dying. We went along with their beliefs. Raja suggested that we stay there that night and that they would organize a welcome feast for us, and we could go home the next day. We politely declined, saying that people would worry if we didn't return. But we promised to come back tomorrow with more people and bring food with us if that was okay. We mentioned that we could also bring doctors who could check if anyone had any problems, and that we had medicine for most things. They agreed, and five locals accompanied us back to where we first encountered them. We waved goodbye and continued on. "Did they say how many people are in the village?" I asked Bandil. "I understood it to be around 800, about the same as us. I just don't understand how they survived." "They said why: they weren't sinful," Jack interjected. We continued talking for the rest of the hike. "It should guarantee they wouldn't harm us if they believe that," I said. "We can hope so; guerrilla warfare in the jungle doesn't sound appealing," replied Jack.

When we arrived in Bentota, I asked Jack and Bandil to explain the situation to the others and tell them there was nothing to worry about. I had to go to the shuttle and inform Riya and the others, as well as get in touch with Jose. I explained to Jose what had happened, and he wanted to come over to us today and accompany us to the new village tomorrow. He would bring a few participants with him. I further told Jose that the locals were also aware of their village. Everyone was quite startled in the shuttle when I recounted our adventure. But I genuinely believed they were good people; otherwise, they would have made life difficult for us earlier.

"I want to come along tomorrow," said Riya. "Of course you should come; I like when my wife joins me on my business trips." "Anyone else up for a jungle party tomorrow?" Riya asked. The entire medical staff raised their hands, along with a few patients. I laughed, "Take a few people; I think a group of 20-30 would be suitable. Later, we could even invite their whole village here for a big party."

A few hours later, Jose arrived with a delegation of ten people in total. There had been the same enthusiasm in

Madu, but Jose wisely chose a smaller delegation. And the best part was, a woman who could speak Sinhalese was among them. She was an Indian who had studied languages at the University of Colombo, the same university Bandil had attended. Her name was Fatima, and she was one of the participants. We had decided that 20 of us would go: me, Riya, Jack, and, of course, Bandil. Having Jack and me along again was mainly because we had already built trust with them. We also had another doctor besides Riya, two nurses, and the rest were enthusiastic participants. Mike stayed behind with Ra because I wanted them to be there. Ra pouted, trying to look disappointed, though without much success. Everyone had brought small gifts for the children in the village, chosen from their personal belongings. The hunters had shot a large wild boar, which we skewered on a pole to take turns carrying. We also had a few large fish that were cleaned and salted. We went to bed early so we could be well on our way when the sun rose.

23 VILLAGE FEAST

At dawn, our 30-person strong party committee gathered. The wild boar was on the pole, and we agreed to switch the two carriers at short intervals. The boar weighed at least 50kg, so it was no easy task. Mike was on the beach and said, "If I get to come along, I promise to carry it all the way by myself." "You're needed here now, and you'd probably eat it along the way," I replied. Just as we were about to start, Jelena, who was Russian, said, "I just wanted to announce that Dimitri and I are expecting a baby, so in about eight months, we'll need a babysitter." Everyone shouted and congratulated them, "Riya confirmed it yesterday." "Congratulations, that's fantastic news, but are you sure it's a good idea for you to push yourself here?" I asked. Riya laughed, "She's pregnant, not sick." "Okay, okay, I'm not so good at these things," I laughed in response.

We marched off in high spirits; this was news we had been waiting for. At the next village meeting, I would suggest that building a house for Dimitri and Jelena become our first priority. When we reached the spot where we were ambushed last time, Raja and five young men were waiting for us. It was a happy reunion, and Raja immediately commanded two of his men to carry the boar. Down in the village, everyone was waiting for us. The children were much braver now, and our blondest participants received a lot of attention. All the children wanted to touch their hair and asked them to sit down. Then they began braiding and styling it skillfully.

Even though it was still early morning, the cooking of the boar and fish began immediately. They had already set up an assortment of dishes on the ground. I recognized the chicken and most of the fruits, at least. Raja asked me and Bandil to come aside and sit with him, so of course, I took Riya along. We learned a lot from Raja, who was also a good listener; he naturally wanted to hear more about our adventures. Raja wondered if it would be possible to teach them English. I told him we had teachers with us who couldn't speak Sinhalese, but Bandil and Fatima could help with that. With some practical learning, we would eventually be able to understand each other better. The younger children, in particular, would learn quickly.

We also mentioned that we were very interested in their crops, especially rice and its preparation. We noticed they had goats and wondered if they'd be interested in a trade for some pregnant pigs. Sea fishing was something they were interested in in Kotte, as their village was called. They currently fished in the river but had no experience with sea fishing. "We don't have any experience with river fishing, so we'd be happy to exchange knowledge," I replied. Raja went on to explain that the river was rich in crayfish and crabs, which had become rare delicacies back in our time. My mouth was already watering.

Riya asked if it would be okay to do a health check on the children. She also mentioned that she could vaccinate them against the pandemic if they wished. But Raja said it wasn't necessary, as they were good people. We let it go for now, hoping the disease had indeed died out by now. Riya explained the benefits of a vaccination program for children, and he agreed we could start it. "But today is a party," Raja said, "so no needles today." We laughed and agreed.

It was an incredible meal with plenty of food, many very spicy dishes, but delicious. We had almost forgotten how good rice could taste, and it also helped to cool down anything too spicy. Then the familiar pipe went around, and I politely but firmly declined. Riya also declined, saying, "I'm from India; ganja is common there. But I've seen how it can dull people who overuse it. And while there's no risk of me driving today, I'll pass, thanks."

The meal, whether it was lunch or dinner, went on for hours, and just when we were about to burst from eating, the wild boar was served, so we had to dig in again. We were offered some kind of homemade liquor – I don't know if it was made from rice or coconut, but it was strong. After a while, we were all in quite a festive mood. There was music too, drums and a guitar-like instrument. Our young women were enthusiastically courted by the young men of Kotte, while the village's young women were quite reserved, although very beautiful and likely to spark interest among our young men eventually.

As much fun as we were having, we decided to head back to Bentota before nightfall. We agreed that Riya and the medical team would return the next day to check on all the village's residents. I thought Mike, Ra, and maybe a few others might want to come along too. We invited the villagers to visit us as well, but they were still a bit hesitant, wanting to see how things went with us first. And I understood them; if they had been brainwashed for generations into thinking it was a dangerous place, that mindset wouldn't change overnight.

The next day's excursion, led by Mike and Ra, also went well. Three pregnant sows had been brought along, and they managed to walk on their own. In exchange, we received five goats, which we quickly realized worked great as lawnmowers. Although we had to keep an eye on them because they would eat almost anything they saw. But now we had goat milk and could make goat cheese, among other things.

Riya's medical team started the vaccination program, and the younger children began calling her "Doctor Mod." Riya thought it was sweet until Fatima explained that "mod" means "foolish" or "silly." So now Riya was the "silly doctor" who came to poke them with needles. Some fishermen and hunters also joined us to exchange experiences. The hunters in Kotte mentioned that they sometimes heard roaring deeper in the jungle, which they suspected was something larger than a leopard. It could mean that tigers, which had gone feral after the pandemic from nearby zoos, might be around. They said there were plenty of elephants too, sometimes in large herds that would come and eat their maize crops. So far, they had managed to ward them off, but there was a certain level of concern. This was one of the reasons why they were very interested in our guns. However, we explained to Raja that firearms could lead to more trouble and suggested it would be best if they stayed with us. But we promised to help them if they ever had issues with the elephants.

A bigger problem, however, was the monkeys, which could also arrive in large groups and steal everything in sight. They could also become aggressive. Riya explained that if anyone got bitten, they should come to Bentota immediately to get a rabies vaccine. If rabies were contracted and left untreated, it would always be fatal. Everyone in the village also received a tetanus shot. It was surely a sign of trust that everyone came to receive them.

Ra had made a football out of woven vines and was teaching them the rules while kicking it around with them. The children seemed to appreciate organized activities and had a fantastic time with Ra. So, we drew closer to each other and built trust. We also received rice, which we promised to repay once our harvest came in. But food was not in short supply. Nature provided, and it began to feel like Linda had made the right choice when she picked the best possible place to live – Sri Lanka was wonderful.

The purification plant was up and running, and we could move into our house with Riya. The water cistern was in place, allowing us to shower and use the toilet. Flushing the toilet worked by pouring water into the bowl, which then flowed through pipes to the purification plant. The plant was a real engineering feat and had been built large enough to meet the needs of most of the village – at least with the current population.

And the population was set to grow; after Jelena and Dimitri shared their joyful news, four more couples announced within three months that they were expecting as well. The first rainy season arrived in April, bringing heavy downpours that alternated with sunny days. This also meant that house building had picked up pace, as everyone realized it was no longer feasible to sleep in the beach shelters – some of which had even blown away entirely. We already had our second rice harvest underway, and the villagers from Kotte had shown us how to dry and prepare the rice. That was a lot of work as well, but we had daily visits from people from Kotte, and we often visited them, too.

The children had already begun speaking quite a bit of English, and, in turn, we had slowly started to pick up some Sinhalese. We were already able to communicate a little with each other, and now the bravest from Kotte felt comfortable moving around freely in our "poisoned" village. Our "jungle path" between Madu and Bentota was now complete, so it was no longer necessary to walk along the beach unless you wanted to. Walking along the sandy shore could be tiring since the ground was softer and there was no shade from the sun.

So, things looked quite bright at the moment. But one thought had been nagging in the back of my mind. How would everything continue to function in the future? Many people were working incredibly hard with farming, fishing, hunting, animal care, and cooking. At some point, once the novelty wore off, people might begin to resist if some worked harder than others. How would we compensate those, for example, who worked in the fields for 12 hours a day compared to someone who only worked on their own house and then came to collect food without contributing to the community? Or the fishermen who sometimes went out at sunset, returning in the morning, only to find that everyone had taken the fish they brought back. Or someone who slaughtered a pig, did all the work, and then saw others leave with the meat they had prepared.

Switching to a market economy wasn't feasible either. Who would pay the wages, and with what money? On the whole, everything had worked well so far, but were we inevitably heading toward a capitalist society? These were questions we would have to start considering sooner or later. Perhaps it would be a good idea to have a discussion with Raja. Their society seemed to function well, with everyone having a role. I planned to look into how they had organized things and get to the bottom of it.

One day, I took Mike and Bandil with me to Kotte to meet with Raja. Naturally, we were immediately offered food; for them, it was more of a given than a gesture of politeness. Then we walked around and looked at their crops – water buffaloes were something that interested us. Raja promised to help us capture a few and teach us how to handle them. Since they had gone wild, they wouldn't be easy to manage at first. But they would become absolutely essential for us in the future. They were incredibly strong, and with a weight of several hundred kilos, they could easily be used as draft animals for plowing. They could also pull carts between Bentota and Madu if we wanted to trade goods and harvests.

I told him about our village committee and that we'd be holding a meeting soon, and I asked if Raja would come as an honorary guest. We could invite Madu's village committee at the same time, so Raja could explain the system they used in Kotte. Somewhat to my surprise, Raja accepted and said that now that he'd gotten to know us, he knew we were also among the good people. I had now been village elder for over six months straight – not that I'd pushed for it in any way, but apparently, everyone thought Captain John was best suited for the role. It was the same in Madu, where Jose had been village elder the entire time. Admittedly, Jose and I were the oldest in our respective groups, but personally, I didn't think that should be the criterion.

In Kotte, however, it was more like a monarchy; after Raja, his son would take over the duties of village elder, and he was, in a sense, trained and groomed for it throughout his life. So that was settled, and we decided we'd hold the meeting in Bentota the following week. It would be quite a crowd, as we were 20, Madu had as many, and Raja would come with his son. Additionally, Bandil and Fatima would join us as translators.

I was in high spirits as we headed back, convinced that everything would work out. Raja would surely share useful advice on practical matters like the division of labor and the like. We walked back along the jungle path, which now was like a small road with so many people using it. We paused for a moment at the hill roughly halfway between Bentota and Kotte. Everything looked so peaceful – Kotte's village down in the valley and Bentota with its paradise-like beach.

Later that evening, we sat on our new terrace with Riya, eating some fruit. I asked Riya if she wanted a splash of Cheval Regal, which we'd been sipping sparingly to make it last. "Listen, John, the thing is, you'll be sipping that whiskey alone for the next nine months." I hugged Riya, and though we didn't say anything, we cried with joy. "This is huge, Riya. Forget Quasidor, forget Viridis – we're going to have a child." I jumped up and shouted, "We're going to have a child! We're going to have a child!"

Our closest neighbors came rushing over, happy and congratulating us. Within ten minutes, everyone knew about it. Our little house was packed, and the news spread like wildfire. Sure, there were others who were expecting as well, but apparently, everyone had been waiting for this. Mike spoke up, "We might as well share that Ra and I are expecting a child too." I hugged them both. "Why didn't you tell me?" I asked Riya. "Because I'm a doctor and have a duty of confidentiality – I'm not here to satisfy the old men's curiosity," Riya laughed. "What a day – the best day of my life," I laughed.

After a few days, once I'd had some time to process all the news, it was time for our "grand meeting." We decided to hold it on the beach since we didn't yet have a large enough building ready for the purpose. It was still the rainy season, but the showers weren't daily, and it looked like we'd have a rain-free day. We had logs arranged in a circle around a campfire where we could all fit comfortably. Since there would be around 50 of us, a "round table" setup seemed the best solution so everyone could hear each other.

We sent a small delegation to meet Raja and his four companions: his son and two hunters who always carried their bows. Jose's village committee was already there, and they would also spend the night in Bentota. Raja and his companions could do the same if they wished, but I imagined they would prefer to sleep in the beach shelters rather than in the "poisoned" village.

I welcomed everyone to the meeting, with Fatima and Bandil as translators. I asked Raja to start by talking about the work assignments in their village and his role. Raja stood up, and Fatima stood beside him. It was interesting to hear how things were organized; he explained that jobs were often inherited. Sons followed in their fathers' footsteps from an early age, whether they were fishers, hunters, farmers, or otherwise. Women, on the other hand, cared for the family, raised the children, and managed the cooking and washing. It was like the early 1900s in the developed world. I thought this could be a point of conflict for us. Our participants had grown up with gender equality, but how would it play out in practice? Would we hold onto our traditions or revert to more traditional roles? This was sure to lead to lively debates soon.

One area that was indeed within my expertise was punishment. I asked Raja how they handled matters in Kotte if someone broke the law. I'd thought about it a bit, and a prison would be out of the question in our small village. Raja began by explaining that major conflicts were rare, but it was his role to resolve them if they arose. The most common issues were jealousy dramas, which could sometimes get quite intense. Most of the time, it was enough for the parties involved to come to Raja and share their sides of the story. After that, they would try to reach a resolution that satisfied everyone.

The most severe punishment, or at least the threat of it, was banishment from the community. This meant that a person would have to leave the village for a set period. It was a frightening scenario if things came to that. Surviving alone in the jungle was no easy task, and the nights could be terrifying with all the sounds. And the fact that they were quite superstitious certainly didn't help them get a good night's sleep.

24 DEBATE

Though it was already late in the evening, we, of course, served food since we had guests. We had certainly absorbed that much social etiquette by now. Other participants joined once the official part of the evening was over. We began to split into groups that suited us – I was with Jose, Raja, and Bandil, with Ra, Mike, and a few others joining in. Ra mentioned that she had spoken with Riya, who said she was a bit tired and was going to bed. I became worried and asked if everything was okay with her. Ra laughed. "That was exactly the reaction I was supposed to get," Riya had said. It was all new for me, this dad-to-be stuff, so I figured I was allowed a reaction or two.

I told Raja we were going to have a baby. He took my hand in both of his, looked at me, and said, "I knew since yesterday. You'll learn – news travels fast here." "I'm beginning to understand that," I laughed. Of course, we had to celebrate, and out came that pot with something akin to a sweet, rum-like liquor. There were lively discussions all evening, and Jose raised a thought-provoking question. He continued, "What happens if someone commits a serious crime, like murder or rape? It would be quite difficult to have a vengeful person hiding in the bushes who could come back anytime. And what if he took a gun with him?"

At this, Raja took over. "He had heard that, back in the day, on the Maldives, people were punished by being exiled to uninhabited islands. They could end up sitting there for a lifetime or, at the very least, a very long time." The Maldives had thousands of islands to choose from, but Sri Lanka wasn't exactly known for its archipelago. On the other hand, perhaps the whole world was now uninhabited. Maybe, once the boat builders completed a larger fishing boat, we could sail such a person over to India's east coast. That's what the British did when they colonized Australia. We left the idea at the conceptual stage for now and hoped such scenarios wouldn't arise.

After a few hours of lively speculations, we made sure the guests were comfortable in their shelters. Many from Madu's committee also chose to sleep in the shelters. It was a cloudless night with the moon up, and it didn't look like it would rain tonight. Jose had been taking notes in his notebook throughout the evening and came over to me. "Is it okay if I accompany you to your home before I come back here? I'd like to see Riya and congratulate her too." "Absolutely," I replied. "Maybe a little nightcap of that fine Scotch."

We left the beach and headed up the hill toward our house. The path was dimly lit with LED lamps, and the moonlight helped, so there were no issues. Riya met us at the door. "Hey, Jose! Great to see you – come in," she said, giving Jose a hug. "I wanted to come and congratulate you; what fantastic news." We sat down on some chairs we had found among the rubble we cleared; we'd cleaned them up, and they looked quite fresh. As we sat, Jose tore two pages out of his notebook, handing one to me and one to Riya. It read, "Read this but say nothing. Riya, how fast can you remove the chips from our wrists? Respond by writing here." Jose handed over a pen.

"It only takes a minute; we can do it in the clinic next door. But what is this about?" Riya wrote. Jose wrote back, "Remove them first; we no longer need them. I'll explain once they're gone." Riya and I looked at each other, and then we all headed to the clinic.

25 JOSE SPECULATES

In the clinic, Jose took a bottle of rubbing alcohol. He showed us that, once the chips were removed, we should put them in it. I fought the urge to scream, "What the hell is going on?" but I could tell from Jose's expression that he was serious and had discovered something important. Riya made a tiny incision, maybe 5 millimeters, and removed the chip, which was only a couple of millimeters in size. Then she did the same for herself, as if this were something she did every day. Once all the chips were in the jar of alcohol and we were bandaged up, we went over to our side.

"Perhaps you'd like me to explain," said Jose with a smile. "Yes, perhaps," Riya and I replied in unison.

Jose began, "Do you believe in coincidences? I don't. I started thinking about this during our meeting today, and I couldn't shake the thought. I've always been a rational thinker; I calculate, take no risks. Some might think I'm a real bore, a typical engineer, one might say." I started to get a sense of where Jose was going, and a chill ran through me.

Jose continued, "Wouldn't it be an unbelievable coincidence that, on Quasidor, Linda suggested Sri Lanka as the best option for us? And maybe it is – a wonderful place, and everyone seems happy. But that we'd come here and, so conveniently, find that 800 other people have also survived on Earth, living just a few kilometers away? It doesn't add up, regardless of their story about retreating into the jungle when people started dying from the pandemic."

"They were vaccinated against the pandemic," Riya burst out. "It was airborne; there's no place they could've hidden from it."

"Exactly," replied Jose. "It means someone came in advance, vaccinated them, and then released the virus," I added.

"Damn, Jose, now we've got something to chew on," said Riya. "But who – who in the world would come up with such a devilish plan to wipe out 12 billion people, and why?" Jose wondered.

I replied, "Craig Thomas. He had everything in his hands. I asked him to join us when we were about to leave and were a few people short. He excused himself with something about high blood pressure or something."

"He was one of the healthiest 50-year-olds I've ever met," Riya replied.

"What a bombshell, Jose. We're going to have visitors. I don't know when, but it's going to happen. And how many other oases has he vaccinated around the world? Surely, several at WSA were aware of this – not many, but enough. They're probably in stasis somewhere, programmed to wake up on a specific date. I'm scared," Riya admitted.

"What bastards. What egotistical, narcissistic bastards. Do they think they're going to stroll in here and say, 'Oh, how nice you have it,' and then just settle in with us?" I responded.

Jose said, "They're murderers. They've wiped out an entire civilization. The question is, what do we do now?

We have no idea where they're in stasis. If we did, I'd go there and open the hatch and strangle them with my bare hands."

"Mike!" I shouted, "he served as Craig's bodyguard; he might have been to some secret locations without knowing what they were."

Riya said, "Let's start there. Tomorrow, we discreetly remove Ra's and Mike's chips and go over this with him. But it's late, and we have a lot to ponder. I think it's best to continue tomorrow."

"You're right," I agreed. "We'll keep this between us for now and then decide whose chips to start removing. I'd prefer to take everyone's out, but that might cause alarm."

Jose added, "If they've woken up, they've already noticed our chips are missing and might realize we're onto them."

26 PUNE

Jose insisted on heading down to the beach to sleep with the Madu group and Raja. I think he simply didn't want to intrude on us. But he promised to show up first thing in the morning, which he did. "I'll go fetch Mike and Ra before they get busy with their chores." They lived just a minute away and were standing outside their little house, saying goodbye with a kiss, when I arrived. "Good morning, you two can keep kissing in my company today – I need you." "Oh," said Ra, "I was going to meet my friends." She was teaching English to a group of 3-5-year-olds from Kotte and called them her friends. "You can play with your friends later; there are others who can help out there."

"I was planning to go to Kotte and see how they catch crabs, but that's fine. The crabs can wait. I'll just tell Joni I'll be there later and then come with you," replied Mike. "By the way, bring Joni with you when you come." "Aye, aye, captain," shouted Joni, running off. "And Ra, you're coming with me," I said. "Aye, aye, cap…" "Enough, that's plenty."

When we got close to the house, I handed Ra a note that told her to stay quiet. She was about to say something in her usual Ra-like way, but I put my finger to her lips and signaled her to go into the clinic. Riya was there, finger to her lips, and gestured for her to sit down. Ra sat quietly while Riya removed the chip and put a butterfly bandage on the spot. Riya dropped the chip into the jar of alcohol and laughed, "Now you can talk." "Damn, that felt good! I don't think I've ever stayed quiet this long," Ra said. "Go to Jose and John – they'll tell you why you were 'tortured' for so long."

Riya saw Mike and Joni coming and went to greet them, going through the same procedure with them. After a few minutes, we were all in the room. We chose to sit on the floor since there weren't enough chairs for everyone.

"Thank you all for coming along so cooperatively. I understand you're all a bit curious, and so are we. Jose, please explain why we're here." Jose recounted what he had told us yesterday, and hearing it in daylight made it sound even more chilling than it had the night before.

"We speculated a bit last night, but we didn't get far. However, we see this as a threat to our idyllic life here. And they could come at any time, and we have no idea what their motives might be," Riya said.

Joni raised his hand. "There was no Viridis; it was a fabricated story. Viridis was too good to be true. Perkele," he finished.

"Perkele?" Ra asked.

"A Finnish curse word," Joni explained, "roughly like 'Satan's grandfather,' a strong expression – sorry."

I responded, "We might need both 'sisu' and 'Perkele' going forward, Joni, so it's fine. But now, friends, we need some rational thinking. What do we do next? We have no idea where they are; they have the whole world to hide in. They're lying there, sleeping as if nothing happened, waiting for us to build a paradise for them."

Mike raised his hand, "I know where they are."

27 METREWAVE

We all gaped, mouths open. "Please, continue, Mike," said Jose.

"Well, as you know, I served as Craig's bodyguard whenever he traveled outside the space center. And he did that often; in the last year, we went to Pune in India at least five times."

"What? Pune in India?" interrupted Riya.

"Yes, Pune in India, specifically to the Giant Metrewave Radio Telescope – a massive area spanning tens of square kilometers. But whenever we were there, he mostly stayed in his villa with his delegation – the same people you, John, met at the round table the first time you came to WSA. I was never allowed inside the villa; I was always instructed to keep watch outside. Mostly, I just saw rich tourists wandering around. Metrewave studies pulsars and other space phenomena, so I never thought much of what they were doing in the villa. They all held high positions at WSA, so I assumed it was important business. I didn't even question why they needed to fly to the other side of the world for meetings. But as a cover, it was brilliant. I mean, Metrewave is world-famous and could easily be linked to Quasidor."

The room fell silent.

"I think you're right, Mike. Thank you. So, what now? Any suggestions?"

Ra spoke up, "I say we go and take them out in their sleep. They wouldn't even feel a thing."

I responded, "First of all, Ra, you're not going anywhere. You're staying here, you're pregnant, and the same goes for my lieutenant. Let's stay calm and think this through. Thanks to Mike, we have a sense of the layout, which gives us an advantage."

Riya added, "I know it too; we went there several times when I was a child. It's only 150 km from Mumbai, my hometown."

Mike raised his hand, "Weapons are a problem. We don't know how armed they are, and we can't bring our own weapons."

"Why not?" asked Jose.

"The weapons are chipped," Mike explained. "The chips are embedded in the metal of each weapon, in random locations as a security measure. If a weapon is lost, it can be tracked. Or if an enemy captures it, we can see where the enemy moves. And we all saw how small those chips are – impossible to find."

Joni said, "So, if they're awake, they can track our exact movements."

"Perkele," said Ra.

"We'll leave it here for now. We can't rush this; we'll continue with our daily routines. I don't want to keep this from the others, but let's plan this out first. In the meantime, start discreetly asking people to come and have their chips removed. You can tell a little white lie, like that my hand got a slight infection, perhaps because the chip doesn't tolerate heat or something. It's not mandatory to remove it, but we don't know if the chip can be used for eavesdropping, so we should be cautious."

"This makes me so sad," said Ra. "I dreamed of Viridis. This place is just as beautiful, but I feel so betrayed, like a child finding out Santa isn't real."

Riya replied, "Yes, it's heartbreaking. I was so happy, and everything felt perfect. And now to find out that people we trusted have fabricated this whole thing – what evil people. We must be extremely careful in everything we do from now on. They're capable of anything. And the worst part of dealing with these kinds of psychopaths is that they don't even realize they've done anything wrong."

28 WHAT WENT WRONG

We speculated for a while about what might have led to the decision to kill the entire world's population. Jose, our "thinker," had a theory that the Quasidor project simply became too big. It was likely intended that Viridis would be populated, but with additional data that came in, it became clear that it wouldn't be habitable after all. Perhaps the disappointment was so enormous that they decided to keep it secret to save their own skins. This was, after all, a project involving tens of thousands of people. Many countries had invested enormous resources into it. Now they would have to bear the blame for the failure, perhaps even face prison. And the disappointment for everyone involved would likely put a stop to space exploration for a long time. So it was easier to continue as planned and cover up the failure. Then, there were those who controlled Linda's programming, so anything was possible.

I asked, "But how did it get to the point where they decided to kill the entire world's population?"

Jose continued, "That's something that must have come up within their inner circle. I imagine it was these five core members, led by Craig, who came up with the idea. This way, they could simulate the entire project to conditions that would closely resemble Viridis."

"With one difference," I added. "They would rise like the Phoenix from the ashes and take over leadership of the project."

"Yes, that's where my thoughts are going. After Quasidor was on its way, they had plenty of time to plan their next steps. I guess they put the oldest in the group into stasis shortly after we left. The last one to spread the virus probably did so about 28 years after our departure. Then they would likely have been awakened at 100-year intervals to minimize risks and then put back to sleep. I'd bet anything there's a bunker-like hideout under the villa where, hopefully, they're still in stasis. If so, we'd have a head start on them."

Riya wondered, "But do you really think there would only be five of them? They all had families as well."

"I'm convinced they sacrificed their families to the pandemic too; they couldn't have told them about this plan. Their families simply wouldn't have understood. It's a bit like when Goebbels' family, at the end of World War II, poisoned their own children before taking their own lives. But in this case, they were too cowardly to end their own lives. No, we're dealing with exceptionally dangerous people who think only of themselves."

Mike said, "We need to get to Pune – and fast. We need to start planning right away."

I said, "Unfortunately, Mike's right about everything. But who would we send there? You're obviously the most qualified, Mike, and Riya would be ideal too, but in this case, it's not an option."

"I'll go with Mike," said Joni. "I completed the mandatory military service in the Finnish army and have always been comfortable in nature."

Mike said, "Me and Joni, then we ask two of Kotte's best hunters to come along; we'll need their skills with the bow. We need to tell Raja about our plan. He'll agree once he hears we're threatened."

"We need to start removing everyone's chips – it's impossible to keep this a secret any longer. Can you manage it in a day, Riya?"

"Easily," said Riya. "All the medical staff can handle it."

29 PLANNING PUNE

The de-chipping was done in record time – it was such a minor procedure that not even a stitch was needed. Just cleaning and a bandage. Afterward, we began gathering people in groups to inform them about the events and our theory. Everyone understood the necessity of our plan, and many were so furious they wanted to join the operation. But we stuck to Mike's plan that he, Joni, and two of Kotte's hunters would carry out the mission.

Next, we had to tell Raja about all this and see how he would react, given his belief that "good people" survived. So, Mike, Joni, Bandil, and I went to Kotte. They immediately began setting up food for us, but we politely declined, explaining that we had something serious to discuss. Raja looked concerned and asked us to sit down. Bandil explained the situation, with occasional input from us. We had started to understand Sinhalese reasonably well, too.

Raja looked truly furious, then shouted some commands, and two hunters appeared. Raja was very animated as he explained the situation to them, and a spark lit in the hunters' eyes. Raja said, "They are ready to set off immediately and destroy those who seek to ruin our paradise."

"Thank you, Raja," I said, "but we need to do some planning first, and Mike and Joni need lessons in using the bows." We explained that our weapons weren't usable due to the chips. We had printed a map of India in the shuttle and showed where Pune was located. The boat builders had constructed a fishing vessel that would be ready any day, sail-powered and large enough for eight people. With favorable winds, reaching the Indian coast wouldn't take long. After that, it would be a 1,500 km trek on foot. Mike estimated they could cover 50 km per day.

Dilan and Gayan, the hunters, suggested they could easily walk 100 km in a day, but Mike thanked them for their enthusiasm and explained that 50 km was a long distance in the heat. So, it would take about a month to reach Pune, and, after a hopefully successful operation, another month to return to the Indian east coast, where the fishing boat would camp and wait for them.

We decided they would set off in a week. Dilan, Gayan, Joni, and Mike would undergo intense training with the bows, and Mike promised to teach them how to neutralize enemies bare-handed. Equipment would mainly consist of bows and knives; the element of surprise was everything, as they wouldn't stand a chance in open combat since the enemy would likely be heavily armed.

We thanked Raja for his understanding and support for the mission. There was much to consider before departure; they couldn't carry too much. Riya prepared a first aid kit, including materials for stitching larger wounds, and demonstrated the process. We had plenty of dry rations from Quasidor, and there would likely be game if they got tired of the rations. They also had water purification tablets that could make almost any brackish water drinkable.

It was an exciting week, and the expedition members were treated like superstars throughout the village. Nearly everyone from Madu came to meet them and offer their support. Failure wasn't an option, and we hadn't even considered the consequences of such an outcome.

30 LAUNCH

I went down to the beach where the newly built sailboat was to be launched for a short trial sail. If everything went well, the boatbuilders had been under a bit too much pressure. It was a very simply built boat, essentially a catamaran – about 6 meters long, with two poles connecting to the pontoon, carved to be as streamlined as possible. A sail was attached between two masts, with a sail area of about 5x4 meters, allowing it to reach respectable speeds in favorable wind. We estimated the journey would take about a day; the closest point on India's east coast was around 300 km away. But with a strong tailwind, it could take only 16-20 hours.

We pushed the boat into the water, which was no problem with about 1,000 people there to watch and offer helping hands. Ra insisted on joining the two boatbuilders for the maiden voyage. Mike, of course, protested but had to give in, as usual. Her argument was that it brings good luck to have a woman on a maiden voyage, and double luck if she's pregnant. No one had ever heard such an argument before, but we laughed until tears ran down our cheeks.

I had promised to teach Ra to swim, but she beat me to it; after half an hour in the water on the first day, she was swimming like a fish. Ra was undoubtedly the most popular person in all of Bentota – everyone loved her and her quick wit. Even when she visited Kotte, she had to be careful as all the kids would come running to hug her. They'd even made up a song about Ra, which they sang at every opportunity.

We got the boat into waist-deep water, and the boat-builders hoisted the sail. We released the boat, and it took off at a good speed; everyone applauded and cheered, with Ra sitting at the bow, waving and beaming like the sun. After an hour's sail, they returned and confirmed that it had exceeded all expectations.

I pulled Mike and Joni aside and asked how long they needed for their preparations. "We leave tomorrow morning," said Mike. "We don't have any time to waste. We're not as skilled as Dilan and Gayan with the bows, but we figure that over a month, we'll have plenty of breaks during the marches to use for training."

"Excellent," I replied. "It's best if Dilan and Gayan sleep here on the beach tonight so we can leave at dawn," added Joni.-

The sun had not yet risen over the eastern horizon but was already giving a bit of light. The boat was already in the water, held steady by several people in the gentle waves. It was now being loaded with the expedition's supplies, which were minimal. Each person had a small backpack, a bit of provisions, though they were counting on hunting along the way. They would likely find fruit along the journey too. They brought eight bows with them, along with plenty of arrows sharpened to do significant damage.

It was a diverse group setting off on this expedition. Besides them, a fisherman and a boatbuilder were there to handle the boat, as well as the muscular and agile Dilan and Gayan. Mike looked enormous beside the Sinhalese men, and Ra clung to him, unwilling to let go as she pounded his broad chest. "If you don't come back, I'll come and get you," she said between sobs.

Joni was the calmest of the four, but I knew that if needed, he'd bring out his Finnish "sisu" spirit and then… *Perkele*. Joni also stood out – white-haired with blue eyes, tall and muscular, he'd become quite popular with the young women in Kotte. I guessed we'd soon see a cross-border romance blossoming there.

We waved off the expedition, and the wind filled the sails, and soon they were well on their way. Riya and I went up to sit by the palm trees to watch them for as long as we could. After a while, Ra came and wedged herself between us, showing that now "mom and dad" would need to look after her. We both put our hands over her shoulders and comforted her by stroking her hair. Riya said, "You can come stay with us now until Mike returns." "Thank you, I don't think I'd dare sleep alone right now. Is that okay, Captain?" I kissed her on the forehead and said, "Of course."

The 6-meter-long catamaran moved at a good speed. Roger, the fisherman, estimated that they were going about 11 knots, and if the wind held, they'd reach Uvari Beach on India's southeastern coast by midnight. Space was tight, so everyone stretched as best they could. Though it was a bit uncomfortable, everyone enjoyed the experience. A pod of dolphins followed us for a while until they grew tired and left, but they came close enough for us to touch their rough skin. By sunset, we could see India's silhouette in the distance. Although the wind had calmed slightly, we'd likely arrive around midnight. We planned to camp overnight and in the morning, the catamaran would head back to Bentota. In seven weeks, they'd return, and hopefully within a week after that, we'd meet them there.

After a few hours, we heard waves crashing against the shore, signaling our arrival. It was a sandy beach as expected, based on the maps we'd studied in the shuttle. We jumped off the boat, dragged it far up onto the beach, and set the anchor in the sand to ensure it wouldn't drift away if the tide rose overnight. We built a small campfire and lay down in a circle around it, sore from the uncomfortable crossing. We ate some of our rationed food with little appetite, while Gayan and Dilan refused to try the bland rations and ate dried fish instead. We soon fell asleep under the starry sky, exhausted but with the first leg of the journey complete.

The sun woke us, and we began preparing for departure. We pushed the boat off, and although it now had a bit of a headwind, it handled the necessary tacking maneuvers well with its large, stable rudder, and soon they were well on their way as the sun rose.

We spread out the map and set our course with the compass, eager to start the long journey ahead. After a few hours, it became very hot, so we took a break, estimating we'd covered about 14 km at a good pace. But we realized we'd need two more legs of at least the same length. We began to understand that 100 km a day was an unrealistic goal, but we'd try to reach the 50 km target that Mike had planned. Mike was our obvious leader, and he was constantly alert, as if we were on patrol in enemy territory. Hopefully, the enemy was exactly where we expected them to be.

31 RAILWAY

After walking a few kilometers on the next leg of our journey, we came upon a railway track. It didn't run exactly in our intended direction, but we decided to give it a try since there wasn't much vegetation on it. The track went more directly north, while we needed to go northwest, but we could adjust our course westward at any time. Our pace increased significantly as the ties were in good condition, and once we got into a rhythm, we became so enthusiastic that we even jogged for short stretches.

After a while, when Dilan was leading, he signaled for us to stop. A few meters ahead, a king cobra had noticed us, raising its upper body and spreading its hood majestically. We instinctively drew our bows from their back holsters, but Dilan just laughed. He signaled for us to back up a few meters, which we did, and the cobra quickly slipped away from the tracks into the vegetation. He explained that snakes never want to confront humans; if we show we aren't after it and back off a bit, it will leave. If it has the chance to escape, it will.

"You're welcome to continue leading," said Joni. Laughing and relieved, we continued on our way. There were plenty of snakes now that humans had been absent from their lives for so long. We were guests in their territory. But we learned to live with them, and if we got bitten, we had a universal serum with us. It would save our lives but could slow us down considerably, as it might still be very painful and, in the worst case, lead to a serious infection.

We took a break, and Gayan climbed up a coconut tree, agile as a monkey, cutting down about ten ripe coconuts. With practiced skill, they opened the coconuts and handed each of us one. It tasted fantastic – sweet and refreshing at the same time. We used our knives to cut out the meat inside. The refreshing pause created an almost euphoric feeling. It gave us much more energy than just drinking water, and there was no shortage of coconut palms. There was also a shorter variety of palm where we didn't even need to climb; we could easily reach them. These were a bit smaller and slightly sweeter.

Mike joked, "If I were a coconut, I'd move to India in a heartbeat."

By evening, as we began to set up camp, we saw we had covered about 60 km that day. We knew that after a few days, we'd reach forested areas, and Bandipur National Park lay in our path. There, we were more likely to encounter tigers. If there were a few hundred tigers in the area 400 years ago, it was easy to imagine they had multiplied over the years. We hoped, however, that they'd be as wary of humans as people had said.

Other potential dangers included elephants, monkeys, bears, wolves, and wild dogs, to name a few. We decided to build a large fire to keep any animal visitors at bay. We also kept our bows and knives within reach in case we had any uninvited guests. We all felt the vulnerability of how small we were in the grand scheme of things, almost like when we were in space. Gayan and Dilan hadn't been there, but they likely felt the same way. With total darkness around us, every jungle sound had us on high alert. But we were exhausted from the day's trek, and it didn't take long before we fell asleep. We had set up our campfire between the train tracks and slept there, knowing it was unlikely a train would come.

32 WAITING

In Bentota and Madu, we tried to carry on with our daily routines, though the anticipation was high. We had drawn a large map of India and marked a red line each day on it, indicating 50 km of progress. Ra and everyone else followed it closely, and the map hung outside our door. People from Kotte also came daily to check the map. In reality, I had no idea how far they'd actually traveled, but it seemed to bring some comfort to see that the journey was "moving forward." I performed my role as the "map master" and answered questions with the same response: "We don't know anything; we have no contact with them. This is just the original plan. Let's hope they're doing well." They could have been eaten by tigers, stepped on a landmine, or anything else. But I kept my expression calm and stayed positive, especially for Ra, who was a nervous wreck and needed a lot of support.

It had now been fourteen days, and I estimated they were about halfway to Pune. If all went well, they could be back in seven weeks. We began to have a surplus of food, as the harvests had exceeded all expectations. It was the same in Madu, and we considered planting something other than rice in the next season. We stored the surplus as best we could, though we were starting to have a bit of a rat problem. Kotte could take as much as they wanted, but they weren't in need either. So, we were planning to cut back on production; we had too much grain, and the same was true for the pigs and chickens. We worked closely with the agronomists, who understood this better. The same went for fishing – we were essentially catching as much as we could handle. The oceans had recovered over 400 years, and sea turtles were plentiful, even laying eggs where people were sunbathing. We had no reason to collect turtle eggs as long as we had chickens.

Now that food was under control, we had more time to excavate and expand the ruins in Bentota. Everyone had found homes, and we had even opened a temple or, perhaps more fittingly, a meditation house. It was beautifully situated on a hill, a bit removed from the usual buildings. It was a place for quiet reflection or, for those who were religious, a place to pray. We agreed it would be open to all, equally important regardless of one's beliefs, and no religious symbols would be displayed. People could believe what they wished, but Jews, Christians, Muslims, Buddhists, and everyone else were simply to get along here.

I would go there myself sometimes when I wanted to think; it was far enough from the beach that you couldn't constantly hear the sound of the ocean. Life was becoming almost too perfect, with our only worry being the four brave souls on their mission, hopefully to secure our future. There was always the chance that we were being paranoid and that our ideas didn't align with reality. But Jose's presentation of the situation seemed accurate – there were just too many coincidences.

One morning, two young men came and knocked on the door, asking if they could speak with me. "Of course, come on in," I said. I remembered their names were Masud and Aramis, originally from the Middle East.

"We'd like to speak with you alone, Captain John," said Masud.

"That's fine; I was just heading to the clinic," Riya replied. "I'll come along and help," Ra added.

I invited them to sit down and asked if something had happened. They shifted nervously before starting. "Well, we're not sure if this is forbidden…" Aramis began.

Masud added, "Yes, it's that we care for each other, and we were wondering if that's a problem."

"You mean that you're homosexual?" I asked. They both nodded, somewhat embarrassed.

"Why would that be forbidden or a problem?" I wondered.

"Well, we understood that the mission's purpose was primarily to populate Viridis," Masud explained.

"I see what you mean, and I imagine you come from countries where homosexuality is a taboo. But I assure you that you are just as valuable to us as every other participant. It's true that the expedition wouldn't have lasted many generations if we had sent only 1,600 men, right? So, you understand why there were 800 men and 800 women, but homosexuality exists naturally among both men and women. So, live as you wish and be happy together; it's perfectly natural."

They both brightened, visibly relieved, thanked me, and left, smiling. Later, I told Riya about their visit. "Alright," she said, and that was that.

Conflicts among the members were rare, and Kotte's presence had significantly reduced the pressure to find a partner as quickly as possible. However, many couples had already formed and were working on their new homes, and we now had about ten couples who had announced they were expecting. So far, the teachers had been busy educating Kotte's children, but soon we'd have our own children to teach, which would surely keep them even busier in a year or so.

There were also a few people who had "moved" between Bentota and Madu, which was perfectly fine. We were thinking about many things for the future, including ideas like cafes and restaurants. It would indeed be relaxing to go out to eat. But who would cook, wash dishes, and serve, especially for free? It was a good idea, and it might work as a volunteer-based, rotating system.

Currently, there was no currency. We had received items from Kotte, such as fabrics, spices, tea, and even coffee they grew, as well as tobacco leaves. In exchange, we gave them sea fish, which they were also learning to catch, and pigs, though their pig farming was doing well. So, there was no shortage, but if we introduced a monetary system, we could soon find ourselves in a "vicious" cycle. These were issues people hadn't thought about in thousands of years.

Could it really be as simple as it was now? Coming from a capitalist society, where money was everything for a comfortable life, made it feel challenging. And where was all our bureaucracy? Unthinkable – no bureaucracy! How could one live that way? I laughed at my own thoughts. Time would tell; as we grew, maybe our small village committee wouldn't be enough.

I went to the clinic to hug Riya and feel her belly. Ra wanted me to feel her belly, too.

33 THE FINAL DAY

We had now been walking for four weeks, sometimes through dense jungle, other times across savannas with sparse vegetation. Where the jungle slowed us down, we made up for it on the savannas and on some roads that weren't overgrown. Tomorrow, we would enter the Metrewave area and reach the villa we were searching for in the afternoon. Of course, we had no intention of just knocking on the door and saying, "Long time, no see. How's it going?" They were probably armed, but we had one advantage: at least for now, we believed they were unprepared for our arrival. But we would need to approach cautiously, staying hidden to observe the house and check for any movement.

We set up camp for the night but didn't start a fire this time. Even though we were still tens of kilometers away, there was a small chance they might be hunting or detect the smell of smoke or see the fire. We had encountered plenty of wildlife; once, we glimpsed a tiger in the distance, but it quickly retreated into the vegetation. A larger herd of 50-60 elephants once spotted us. They paused and stared at us, with the lead male stepping forward as if to assert, "This is our territory." There were a couple of hundred meters between us, so we changed direction and made a wide circle around them, and they lost interest.

We had all learned quite a bit of both Sinhalese and English and could already communicate well with each other. But tomorrow could bring situations none of us had experienced before. It was possible we might have to kill people, likely in brutal ways. They probably had machine guns, while we only had bows and knives. Now that we were skilled with the bows, we almost felt that we'd rather be hit by a bullet than an arrow. The arrowheads were razor-sharp and flared out in a way that made them look like miniature, unopened umbrellas. If hit by one, it was almost impossible to remove without causing severe damage. These arrows were designed for hunting deer and wild boar; if the shot was well-placed at close range, the animal died quickly as the arrow sank deep into the flesh.

We didn't plan much yet; first, we had to scout the area. Mike said the area might be overgrown, making it hard to find. Mike also hoped that the massive radio telescopes hadn't all collapsed; with a diameter of 45 meters, they could aid our navigation. After our "midnight snack" of space rations and dried fish, we lay down to sleep, which was considerably more uncomfortable without a central fire.

We woke after a rough night's sleep and prepared for our final trek, hopefully, with another to come when it was time to return home. Mike gathered us in a circle, extending his hand, and we all placed our hands on his. He prepped us like a coach before a crucial game: "Today, we have to stay alert the entire time. We'll walk with 10 meters between us. I'll lead, keeping my eyes forward. You keep watch on the sides but keep one eye on me at all times; I'll signal if you need to take cover or spread out. Good luck to us all."

We set off, and for the first time on the journey, we began to realize how serious this was. After about two hours, we saw one of the telescopes, enormous and completely overgrown. But it was intact, and Mike explained that they were spread out over a large area. We weren't near our target yet, but this would help us find the villa. The villa might be collapsed, but we were more interested in what might lie beneath it – likely a bunker equipped with all the technology needed to sustain long-term stasis.

We walked for another hour until Mike raised his hand; we heard it too – voices. Mike gestured for us to wait. He crawled forward in a way only someone with military training could manage, using the tall vegetation as cover. We sat and waited, hearing snippets like, "Put those under the others," "Hand me that," as if they were loading something.

After a few minutes, Mike crawled back, drenched in sweat. "We need to hurry – they're loading an electric helicopter. If they take off, we're done."

"A helicopter?" Joni asked.

"Yeah, they probably had one in the bunker that they've assembled. We need to move now."

We approached from a slight elevation and were maybe 20 meters from the helicopter when we dropped to the ground. "I don't see Craig," Mike whispered. "He's probably in the bunker; I'll go deal with him. There are four guys loading the helicopter – can you handle them?"

We nodded, though probably not with the most confidence. The rifles were likely already loaded into the helicopter, but each had a holstered pistol. Surprise was now everything. We took good positions, indicating who would shoot whom. If we all hit our targets, which was likely, one would remain, and we'd have to eliminate him before he reached his pistol. We drew our bows; three fell, screaming in pain. No doubt Craig would have heard that if he were in the bunker.

The one who wasn't hit was Ralph Wiggum, whom Joni had met once on the departure day. He made a run for the helicopter before we could draw our bows again. Joni threw himself at him, pulled open the helicopter door, grabbed Ralph's hair, and began pummeling him with his fists, shouting "Perkele!" between punches until Dilan came up behind him and slit Wiggum's throat. Joni, shaking, stood up, muttering, "Thanks."

Outside the helicopter, Gayan had slit the throats of the other three, as if slaughtering a pig.

Mike went down the stairs toward the bunker, where Craig approached him with a pistol in hand. "Mike, I hope you come in peace. I saw on the monitor what happened out there. I hope you're not here for me." Mike stared down the barrel of the gun. "What the hell were you thinking? You killed the entire world's population."

"Mike, you must understand – it was inevitable. After you all left, Earth was in chaos. It was one giant war, everyone fighting each other, and we had to react. You know we had a backup plan for everything. Now we can rebuild Earth, just like you did on Viridis. What do you say, my loyal Mike? You and I can lead the whole world. You could even be president, and I could be your advisor." Craig lowered the pistol and approached Mike. "Let's forget everything and start over, doing it all right this time – you and me."

Mike stepped forward and embraced Craig. "It'll be alright, you'll see," Craig said.

They stood there, still hugging, when Mike said, "I have a message from John and Riya." Craig felt a knife plunge into his stomach and twist. Everything went dark for Craig as life drained out of him for good. Mike pulled out the knife and wiped the blade on Craig's pants. Engraved on the blade were the words: "To our friend Mike, Christmas 2173, John & Riya."

We all entered the bunker and washed off the blood. We sat down for a moment to collect our thoughts. Mike was the first to speak: "There's a lot of technology here we could take back and use. But my suggestion is that we leave it all here. Same with the weapons – let's throw everything in the bunker and burn it. Our lives are good now; why complicate it?" We all nodded in agreement.

"Should we burn the helicopter too?" Joni asked.

Mike replied, "We marched here, and it worked fine. But no way are we doing that march again. I know how to fly it. Let's land on the beach as victors. We'll be home tomorrow." We cheered and quickly started dragging the bodies into the bunker, tossing in the weapons from the helicopter as well. Then we filled the bunker with all the flammable junk we could find until it was packed to the ceiling. We set it alight, making sure the fire took hold. We stood outside for a while, watching flames shoot out from the bunker entrance.

We climbed into the helicopter, now emptied of everything else. Joni asked, "And you're sure you know how to handle this?"

"Sure, sure – we'll see," Mike laughed.

Dilan and Gayan looked terrified, and we completely understood. We flew about 700 km before needing to land to recharge the solar panels. Mike said we'd have to stay overnight here and recharge throughout the morning, but after that, we should be able to make the rest of the journey and be home by tomorrow afternoon. We could have slept in the helicopter, but we chose instead to build a campfire and talk about the day's events.

Everything had happened so quickly; in a matter of minutes, we had eliminated our opponents. They were completely surprised – perhaps that's the thing about intelligent people; they underestimate everyone else. Had we arrived even a few hours later, it would have been too late. Jose had said he didn't believe in coincidences, and this had been a close call. And what if Jose hadn't figured this all out? What would our world have looked like then?

Dilan asked, "What was that word you shouted in the helicopter when you hit him? Perk…?"

"Perkele," Joni replied. "A strong word we had in Finland. I don't even remember saying it – it came from somewhere deep inside, somehow."

We got up in the morning and looked at the helicopter, still finding it hard to believe it was real. The batteries needed to charge a little longer. Then Mike said, "We have a bit of a problem. When we get home, we might get shot by our own people – they'll think it's Craig and his gang."

"I'll take care of it," Joni said with a laugh.

34 TWENTY-EIGHT DAYS

It had now been 28 days since the expedition started. On our map, the red line had reached Pune. More people than ever gathered to speculate, some sending thoughts to them, and the believers perhaps offering prayers. Otherwise, we were completely helpless in this situation. I couldn't help but imagine the worst in my mind. We had our weapons hidden on the beach, ready in case of an invasion – Craig and his gang wouldn't get away easily if they dared to come here. And what would have happened to our four expedition members if they showed up without them?

I asked everyone to go about their daily tasks, even though it wasn't really my place to do so. I just didn't want them hanging around our house. Ra was having a particularly hard time today; she stayed close to Riya, trying to help in the clinic and the shuttle hospital. People tended to gather on the beach before sunset, not only to meet up but also to watch the spectacular sunset. There were nearly 1,000 of us on the beach when we heard it – the sound of helicopter rotors. Instinctively, people took cover behind rows of palm trees and other vegetation. "Damn it," I muttered to myself, holding Riya close. The hunters took their positions, rifles ready.

The helicopter turned north when it was about a kilometer away. Then it banked and came south, flying parallel to the beach, about 200 meters offshore and maybe 50 meters up. The hunters kept it in their sights the whole time. Then we saw it and understood why they were flying sideways along the beach. Behind the helicopter was a banner that read "Perkele."

I ran out onto the beach, and Ra appeared too, understanding what it meant. "It's ours! It's ours!" we shouted. People began emerging onto the beach where we were standing, jumping and shouting, and Ra openly cried out in joy. The helicopter landed, and out jumped our expedition heroes. The excitement and celebration were indescribable. It took a long time before we could even talk to Mike, Joni, Gayan, and Dylan, they were so surrounded by people.

After we heard their report of what had happened, I gave orders – yes, this time, I really did give orders, knowing no one would object. "Someone go to the shuttle and contact Madu. Tonight, it's going to be the biggest party Bentota Beach has ever seen, so make sure they all come here! And Gayan, send someone to Kotte to tell them the news and invite everyone to the celebration. And bring as much homemade liquor as they can carry! We'll slaughter a couple of pigs and chickens and get the food preparations started."

The atmosphere was euphoric, and everyone shared in the joy. Ra was perhaps the most hugged and embraced, as everyone knew how hard she had taken it. By that evening, we were likely 2,500 strong, thoroughly enjoying the coconut liquor. When we set up the stereo system we'd brought from the shuttle, people began chanting, "DJ John, DJ John!" I started thinking of the perfect song for the night. Then I found one from the 1980s – over 500 years old by now – a song on a memory stick. The band was called Opus, and the song was "Live is Life." It got everyone going, and everyone joined in the chorus.

I stood with Riya, looking out over the beach. "Do you think we'll get to live happily for the rest of our lives with our daughter?" I asked.

"I hope I'm not disappointing you," she replied. "But it's going to be a son."

I put my arm around her shoulder, looked out over the ocean, and smiled.

35 ONE YEAR LATER

It had now been a year since the successful expedition returned, and much had changed, of course. We had an 8-month-old son named Raj, a lively little guy who was born traditionally in the shuttle. I was there for the birth, and Riya suggested that it might be better if I sit out the next one. I had been far more anxious than Riya and was just as exhausted as she was by the end. Ra and Mike had their daughter a few days later, and the tough soldier Mike also got "banned" from any future births. We had tough women here!

Many children were born that first year, and things had gone well so far. The people from Kotte also came to the shuttle for childbirth, which had significantly reduced infant mortality compared to home births. We were also able to vaccinate the children against the most common childhood illnesses. But there was much to think about regarding infrastructure. What should our future look like?

After some pressure, I agreed to become the "village elder," following the same system as in Kotte. I accepted the role on the condition that it would be re-evaluated every year. It was not a position I aspired to, nor did I want it to be passed down to Raj when I grew too old for it. Jose became the "village elder" in Madu, a natural choice. We still had our village committees, which rotated regularly, but we hadn't yet found a solution to the big issues, perhaps because everything was functioning well enough for the moment.

People took responsibility and helped each other; there was no reason to be envious of someone else's house. Anyone was free to renovate or build a new one, and materials were plentiful. Interests and roles were distributed naturally: we had medical trainees and people interested in healthcare, and many enjoyed working with animals and farming. With help from Kotte, we captured and tamed some water buffalo, which were a great help in the fields.

Our firearms were put away, and we used bows for hunting instead. We didn't hunt much, though, as we had plenty of pigs, goats, chickens, and fish. Many people from Kotte joined in adult education, where we learned about fabric-making for clothes, blankets, and more. Everyone began to master Sinhalese at least passably, and, in turn, Kotte's people were learning English. Joni found a partner in Kotte and spent more time there than in Bentota.

Maybe we'd continue as we were for a while, but I guessed that in 50 years, when Earth's population had grown beyond the current 2,500 people, we'd need some kind of currency. What would happen when there were 10,000 of us and we'd likely start spreading out? Maybe some people would want to explore and colonize other places. Perhaps someone would want to return to their homeland or simply broaden their horizons. Everything was possible for us now, and we shared a planet we needed to protect and avoid the mistakes of our ancestors.

It might be good to delve into history and see where things went wrong. Was it only due to religions? "You have the wrong god, so you must be killed" – we had surely learned enough not to go down that path. Tribal wars were also common, but why? In ancient times, there was land and game enough for everyone. Or is humanity just too greedy to help one's neighbor? But a world without bureaucracy and politics should be possible as long as it remains small-scale.

I tattooed a phrase on my arm long ago, which says in Latin, *"Ubi bene ibi patria,"* meaning roughly, "Home is where things are good." I think it fits my life quite well at the moment.

36 EPILOGUE

Now, two years after our arrival in Sri Lanka, daily life had begun to settle in. After our incredible adventures, life had calmed down, and after the initial excitement, we all settled into a more tropical rhythm – more active in the morning and a few hours before sunset. It was simply too hot in the middle of the day, and even our animals sought shade in the shelters we built. We now had about 30 dogs that panted through the day and became more active as the sun set. They were valuable as both companions and guard dogs, keeping a watchful eye on the monkeys and deterring them from getting too close. The veterinarians had vaccinated the dogs against rabies, treated them for parasites, and fed them all they wanted. You could call them happy "street dogs."

Our crops exceeded all expectations, and we had an abundance of rice. As we expanded the cultivated area, we needed to reduce the rice planting. Sweet potatoes grew well in the tropics, too. We also planted large fields of fruit trees like mango, papaya, lime, and my personal favorite, pineapple. We had plenty of spices, with chili and pepper as the main ones. By now, everyone had found a place to call home – some lived alone, others with friends, or had already started families. Many had lovely gardens where they grew small plots for personal use. Our infrastructure steadily improved, though some parts began to show signs of wear. For instance, our tractor had nearly exhausted its supply of spare parts, so we decided to use it sparingly to make it last longer.

We had tamed more water buffalo, which were incredibly useful in the fields and also as draft animals on the now well-built road between Bentota and Madu. We constructed wagons for transporting goods – and people – between villages. They didn't exactly move at rocket speed, but we were rarely in a rush. The helicopter the expedition had brought back had become unusable due to the need for regular maintenance. After its arrival, Mike made a few trips to survey nearby areas from above, which gave us valuable information. But we decided it was now too risky to use, so we parked it near the space shuttle for future generations to see. At least they'd have a head start compared to the early attempts of inventors like Leonardo da Vinci.

Our talented engineers worked diligently on recycling the metal and plastic humanity had left behind – more than enough to last our lifetimes. But everything took time, and that was one thing we had in abundance.

At home, life had completely changed since Raj was born. Now a big boy, he had already started walking on his own. He was well aware that he would have a sister in seven months and checked his mom's belly daily to see if it had grown. Jose and Yong Kodcharen had been together for a while, and Yong was also pregnant. There was a baby boom in our villages, and spirits were high.

We traveled to Madu to visit them. We rode in the large wagon our skilled carpenters had built, pulled by two water buffalo. We brought tea leaves, coffee beans, and tobacco leaves we'd received from Kotte. There was such an abundance that we often gave away what we had too much of. I knew we'd return with a wagon full of goods, too. Riya and I would, of course, visit Jose and Yong. The journey took almost two hours as the buffalo leisurely plodded along the jungle path. About ten people rode in the wagon, but it was no trouble for the tireless buffalo.

As usual, our conversation drifted to politics – or the lack of it. What kind of system did we have, really? Jose put it simply: "We're reluctantly chosen dictators with royal status, along with a government (the village council) that must participate until they're replaced."

I laughed. "That's one way to look at it, but everything's working so far. It seems to work with a small number of people. But what about the future when we're significantly more?"

Jose looked thoughtful and said, "Maybe that's the solution – to have smaller communities with the same system. I could see us having another village between Madu and Bentota. We could start building houses there, and anyone who wants to can move in."

"But in the long run, they'd merge with Bentota and Madu, becoming a larger metropolis. We could divide the metropolis into districts, each with its own village elder," I added. "But we likely won't be around when the challenges grow that big – if they even do. What's most important is that we raise our children, and they theirs, to respect others and help wherever it's needed. And as I've said, we have an entire planet at our disposal. For the long-term survival of humankind, I think it's good if people eventually migrate from here as well."

"I'll drink to that," Jose said, and we clinked glasses filled with coconut rum mixed with pineapple juice. We sat on Jose's terrace, which also had an ocean view. Our wives were in a lively discussion about child vaccinations. Jose and I sat quietly, looking out over the sea – silent in the way only good friends can be, when everything feels just right.

I have always believed in humanity's goodness, and now it feels like I was right. What could possibly go wrong?

INNEHÅLLS-FÖRTECKNING